The Secret Staircase

by

Melanie Jackson

Version 1.2 – October, 2011

Discover other titles by Melanie Jackson at
www.melaniejackson.com

ISBN 978-1468186185

Printed in the United States of America

Chapter 1

Kelvin was dead to begin with. There is no doubt about that.

No, I can't do it. I can't plagiarize Dickens. It's a great beginning for this story though....

Let's try again.

My Grandma Mac once told me that a malicious faerie had christened me in my cradle, giving me both brains and insight. Not a bad combination, you might think, but you probably weren't born into a family that was as, shall we say, *salt of the earth* as mine. In my birth family, beauty and good nature were coin of the realm. My parents were simple. Trusting. Gullible. Apt to see life in shades of rainbow pastels when really the situation was very black and white. I was not that way.

Not that I put too much weight on this particular matter now that I am grown and accept that beauty really is only skin deep and that insight and intelligence are useful to my chosen trade. But it had mattered very much when I was a child and certain most days that I was a changeling put on earth to look after my supposed parents.

This story is in part a cautionary tale as well as a fable, so there must be a moral. Perhaps *blood will tell* or *you can run but not hide*. In any event, the sins of the fathers being what they are, when my grandmother had run away from her family and married a traveling man that they objected to, she changed the course of Wendover familial events and destinies. Wild blood entered the line and poisoned it—this is what my grandma said not long before she died. At the time I had thought she was speaking of my grandfather, but now I think perhaps she meant something else as well.

I didn't know Grandma's traveling man, so this part of the tale is all second-hand telling, but I think it's fairly accurate since my mother hadn't the guile to lie about her father and Grandma Mac wouldn't have bothered.

Grandma was the primary breadwinner and the steady influence in her children's lives. Once in a great while, my fly-by-night grandpa would breeze into town, bringing presents for his wife and daughters. He would have a drink or two, watch a little television, and then, once Grandma was asleep or away at her job, he would tell my mother tall tales about this subverted destiny of the high and mighty Wendovers who had thought themselves too good for him, and how he had saved my grandmother from a terrible fate. My mom, being gullible, came to think of my grandma as an unhappy princess kidnapped by the king of gypsies who had fallen in love with her and saved her from her cruel family by marrying her. It was my mother's favorite bedtime story, made more precious because her own mother would never speak of the Wendovers. It was the extra-special secret she shared only with her mostly missing father.

In turn, my mother told me the lost princess stories when I was a child. It was the only story she told me, and I came to think of myself as being lost too—a changeling, as I said. Or maybe cursed. Clearly I didn't belong with my supposed birth family. They were fair and I was dark. My mother had sapphire blue eyes and I had nondescript gray. My parents were small and delicate, and I was tall and sturdy. Handsome, not pretty.

Nor did I belong in that small town, with its small minds and small tolerance for smart girls who acted up in Sunday school and refused to join the choir. I longed to see the ocean and maybe to travel to foreign lands. I spent a lot of time looking at *National Geographic* at the library and feeling I belonged somewhere else.

Perhaps, given Grandma's hostility and reluctance to accept her familial destiny, it was fair that her parents' predictions of a disastrous marriage were proven true, and that she should give birth to two very pretty but empty-headed children, neither of whom sought to make up for this deficit by marrying someone brighter or more sensible than they. Instead the sisters married for what they thought was love and for happiness, and more or less achieved it, though in very different ways.

Fortunately, Holly and Emmett (my mom and dad preferred I use their first names) were both sweet tempered and easy going, so I was able to organize home as I liked and arranged for my education, in spite of their indifference to this matter. Grandma supported me in my desire for college, saving every spare penny she could for my tuition, hoping I would in turn help her at the newspaper when I graduated. Which I did. I couldn't do otherwise when she needed assistance and would never have it from her own children.

I never got the straight scoop on the Wendovers from either my grandmother or my mother. Grandpa, who turned out to be a con man and blackmailer as well as a snake-oil salesman, might have told me about them when I was older, but he had died under questionable circumstances not too long after Aunt Verena was born. My mom was only five at the time, so it is doubtful she knew any more about them than I did.

Things were rough after Grandpa and his ill-gotten gains were no longer adding to the coffers. If anything should have driven my grandmother back to her family, it would have been this, but she stayed resolutely away from Maine, choosing to work as an editor/reporter at a small newspaper just outside Duluth. Though Grandpa Mac wasn't a man to be proud of, my grandmother kept his name in preference to the one she was born with. Her maiden name, Wendover, was almost never spoken of after he died, and when it did come up in her presence, it was never said with affection. Especially when she spoke of her father, whom I came to think of as a Victorian-style tyrant, before forgetting him entirely during the turmoil of my teen years.

My parents didn't understand me or my educational ambitions, but were proud of my accomplishments, and we would probably still be enjoying a comfortable if uncomprehending relationship had my dad not decided to take the advice of a friend and try to improve a new fuel-injection system that blew both my parents to bits on the first test-drive when I was only a year out of college.

My Aunt Verena is dead now too. Kicked in the head by a riding horse she was trying to "return to the wild," if you can believe it. She was survived by her husband, Zach, but as my grandma had pointed out, Zach—unlike my naïve father—was a stranger to both truth and shame. He was, in addition to being a liar who always got caught in the act and was often in jail, kind of ugly. I am speaking in the physical sense though his soul was also far from shiny. His red face was clean shaven but he had a neck beard that ran straight into the pelts on his chest and back. It stuck up out of his shirt and he often looked like he was peering at you out of some kind of tall grass. As a kid I found this creepy. Actually I still find it creepy. I don't see him anymore.

Grandma Mac passed away two years ago, and since Verena and Zach had no children, I am all that is left of our little clan, the last descendant of the runaway princess and the gypsy king.

That I possibly had kin somewhere else never occurred to me. The Wendover stories were largely forgotten in the daily grind of keeping the newspaper afloat, and somehow I had gotten the impression that Grandma was an only princess anyway, so there was no point imagining loving cousins somewhere in Maine. But one day a letter appeared in my mailbox announcing that I was the heir to the Wendover estate, which included a large house on a tiny island and some two hundred and fifty thousand dollars in securities, bonds, and cash. The attorney and author of the letter, Harris Ladd, suggested that I should call his office when it was convenient and we could settle the details of the estate.

I had taken over my grandmother's job at the newspaper, which she had eventually been conned into buying once the first owner was bled dry and decided to retire to Arizona while he still had a shirt on his back. I was making little better than minimum wage for overtime labor while the swirling, sucking, almost bankrupt money pit of false hopes and shattered dreams swallowed most of the revenue it brought in on a good month—and more than that in a bad one—so it was convenient to call at once. After all, I needed a new car before winter and a mortgage if I was going to buy my apartment when it went condo and I was pretty sure I couldn't get a conventional loan. The newspaper was hardly adequate collateral. These days the banks were like a school of fish. Ask for money and they scattered in terror. I didn't really want to take on the debt anyway. Though I hated to admit it, since the paper had been my grandmother's life work, it seemed to me that *The Democrat* wasn't long for this world unless the town's reading population tripled and the economy got a whole lot better and very quickly.

The mild-voiced Mr. Ladd suggested I visit as soon as was possible—the estate would pay, of course.

Go to Maine? Just pack up and go? Could I do that?

I sat at my desk in the empty office and pondered my options. It was 104 degrees and sultry. My only fulltime staff reporter was on vacation getting a facelift, and our only photographer had just broken his leg carrying shingles up to his ex-wife's leaking roof. This was a mixed blessing. Jack of the broken leg and I had tried dating, but he had been too caught up in post-divorce sorrow to be a good companion. Until the divorce, Jack had been the possessor of a sunny temperament which he shared with everyone. After the split, his sun had dimmed and he turned largely inward. A year in, I hoped that an invitation to dinner meant that he was healing, but I had broken off the social connection when I saw which way the ill wind blew. Things were now a little awkward at the office, so a break from each other seemed a good thing.

There was no actual news to report to the wider world of Lakeside except the typical ghastly weather and, in spite of the excitement of the state fair, I was bored out of my skull. So I slapped together a small edition of the Albatross—er, I mean *The Democrat*—that was mainly ads for puppies and kittens and school supplies, with a few puff pieces about the fair's prize-winning sheep and jellies. We usually do twelve pages. That week it was eight. I felt guilty, but I couldn't help it if the social columns were short of weddings, christenings, and funerals. As you may have gathered, when I say that I own a newspaper, that it is a selective newspaper. We report social news like divorces, but without gory details. We print obituaries, but don't mention anything embarrassing about the deceased. Births and weddings are always a favorite. National elections and scandals simply don't exist. Nor does domestic violence, drug use, or drunk driving. There hasn't been a local murder or any unsolved crime in years.

Thanks to that curse of insight and intelligence, I knew better than to mess with Grandma's business formula which had kept the paper in business, but I was slowly dying of boredom. It wasn't that I couldn't face coming to the office the next day. But what about the day after? And the day after that? How long could I do it and not go insane? Would I die at my desk as my grandma had?

At the last minute, I also added a warning in one of the black-bordered boxes we use for obituaries that there had been a death in my family and that I needed to go to Maine for a few days so the next issue might be late. I fired up the ancient wide-format inkjet printer that also needed replacing with something newer, faster, and more reliable, loaded the paper roll, and then I hit the print button. After a moan of complaint, it began printing. Slowly.

Duty done, I turned to the internet and started figuring out the logistics of travel. They were complicated.

It turned out that my inheritance was on Little Goose Island, a small land mass with three houses and a shared dock. It was part of the town of Goosehead, which incorporated Great Goose, Goose Haven, and Little Goose islands. Harris Ladd's offices were located on Great Goose, which is where we met four days later after I had traveled thirteen hours by jet, private plane, and water taxi, all ever decreasingly pleasant modes of travel. The regular ferry only docked on Tuesdays and Fridays, so it being a Wednesday I was out of luck. Hence the water taxi.

There were stares but no offers of help or introduction from the two men on the dock in Great Goose, both of whom had faces that were a decent match for a frying pan and whom I suspected were brothers. As I mentioned, I am fairly tall and athletic looking; probably I seemed well able to carry my own small bag.

The law office was small and squat, as was everything on the one main street, but was antique, built of stone, and on that sunny day, with wild flowers growing out of the cracks in the walls, absolutely charming. There wasn't a single edifice that wasn't charming on an unclouded day. I had a feeling though that in winter it was another matter. Of course, Minnesota does bleak with the best of them, but I suspected that all that gray water probably added another dimension to the feeling of isolation and cold. Oddly enough, I found this exciting rather than off-putting.

Ladd himself was also antique and charming, and almost handsome, in the lean and battered way that some New England men have. Actually, he reminded me of the autographed picture of a young Will Rogers that Grandma Mac had hanging in her den. He was respectability made flesh. When he spoke it was with a slight accent that caused words ending in *r* sound more like *ah*.

"Please, call me Harris," he insisted. "Mr. Ladd is my father."
Fathah.

This informality seemed impossible when he was wearing a bowtie and old-fashioned legless spectacles that clung to the bridge of his sloping nose, so I compromised by not calling him anything.

We settled into the two armchairs on the visitor's side of the desk and Mr. Ladd offered me tea, which I declined. He looked a bit concerned at my refusal and asked if I had had a rough crossing. I spend a little time on myself now that I am nearing forty. Not a lot of time, but I don't come from that magical place where women look beautiful and refreshingly dewy without the aid of some moisturizer and blush, so cosmetic help here and there is necessary. But there is only so much that makeup and a hairbrush can do to repair the ravages of travel. I probably looked as tired as I felt.

I gave in and accepted a cup of tea.

Mr. Ladd was slow to come to business, but I was not perturbed. The chair was comfortable, the tea fragrant, and he would get to the matter in his own good time. There was no need to hurry him and make him think me rude when he seemed so very happy to see me. I gathered from his few words on the subject that finding me had been something akin to the labor of Hercules. Grandma had well and truly covered her tracks when she left Maine. I had only been located when Mr. Ladd began tracking down my grandfather instead. Once he discovered that Grandpa Mac was buried in Lakeside, the rest became fairly easy for a man interested in genealogy. A private eye couldn't find me, but the Mormon genealogists could.

Once Mr. Ladd began legal explanations, he spoke without hesitation. The will was straightforward, but the situation with the Wendover House and environs was not. It turns out that jurisdiction over Little Goose is in dispute. Canada and the United States both claim to own it, though neither claims it very hard and Harris Ladd described it as "an ongoing historical anomaly." I looked it up later and here is what it says in The Treaty of Paris:

And that all disputes which might arise in future on the subject of the boundaries of the said United States may be

9

prevented, it is hereby agreed and declared, that the following are and shall be their boundaries, from the northwest angle of Nova Scotia, that angle which is formed by a line drawn due north from the source of St. Croix River to the highlands; . . . by a line to be drawn along the middle of the river Saint Croix, from its mouth in the Bay of Fundy to its source, and from its source directly north to the aforesaid highlands which divide the rivers that fall into the Atlantic Ocean from those which fall into the river Saint Lawrence; comprehending all islands within twenty leagues of any part of the shores of the United States, and lying between lines to be drawn due east from the points where the aforesaid boundaries between Nova Scotia on the one part and East Florida on the other shall, respectively, touch the Bay of Fundy and the Atlantic Ocean, excepting such islands as now are or heretofore have been within the limits of the said province of Nova Scotia.

Unfortunately, Mr. Ladd explained, this left a few islands in uncertain circumstances.

I asked who islanders paid inheritance and income taxes to, hoping we didn't have to pay both countries, and he said that depended on where the citizen was employed. On Great Goose, the only resident paying taxes to Canada was the lighthouse keeper who worked for the Canadian Coast Guard.

"We have a very able accountant here on Great Goose. Marge Holmes keeps abreast of events and will take care of you when you need help."

This sounded like he was assuming I would stay.

"And if one needs the police or a doctor?" I asked, curious and unable to ignore what might be a good story for *The Democrat*. I was used to living in a small town, but we had a major city nearby. The thought of going to a three-house island was kind of like visiting the edge of the world.

"We have an arrangement with the Haven police department—which is made up of Everett and Bryson Sands. And if you need a doctor, Hillary Abbott is your man—er, woman. She is also here on Great Goose."

"Is there any hope of selling the house?" I asked bluntly, bracing myself for bad news. The economy was hardly hearty in this part of the world and who in their right mind would want to live on an island with only two other houses?

Mr. Ladd looked startled.

"You wish to sell Wendover House?"

"Well, you see I own a newspaper in Minnesota. It would be rather a long commute." Especially given that the paper was on its last legs and I had to work about three different jobs and might have to take on a fourth since my paper boy was threatening to quit if I didn't give him a raise. You know the difference between a small-town editor and Sisyphus? In addition to pushing a heavy weight uphill forever, I also have to pay taxes and rent.

"I'm sorry to sound so surprised. Of course you would want to sell. Just because there has been a Wendover on Little Goose since the late eighteenth century doesn't mean that you would want to stay."

He did not sound convincing and I am not tone-deaf. In fact, I was pretty sure he felt that a failure to stay would be a complete dereliction of duty on my part.

"Wanting doesn't have much to do with it," I replied apologetically and then paused to think about my wishy-washy answer. Did I truly want to stay? "It's the ways and means that are troublesome."

He sat back in his chair.

"I see. But you would like to stay if it were possible? We should think on this. There could be ways to arrange things, creative sources of income that might allow you to hire someone to manage the paper for you."

We. That was kind of nice. His suggestion was not really practical but I appreciated the sentiment.

Certainly there wasn't anything drawing me back to my cracker-box apartment, and only duty to my grandmother's memory forcing me to work every day. I'm not saying this wasn't a strong compulsion, but I was awfully tired of the burden.

However, if I did move here, what would I do? How would I make a living? Two hundred and fifty thousand was a lot of money, but it wouldn't last forever. I would need a job.

"The housing market isn't strong right now and the house does need a little work to make it appealing to outsiders," Mr.

Ladd said. "You know, we have a newspaper here and they are always looking for contributors. It was established in 1820, the year we broke from Massachusetts and became a state."

"No, I didn't know." But I could imagine all too well. I, too, was always looking for contributors who would work for free or very little. I didn't even require that they be able to spell.

"Well then. First of all, it's time to eat. One can't make decisions on an empty stomach." He stood up, removing his strange eyeglasses. He looked younger without them.

"Really? I do it all the time. It's the lot of the owner-publisher of a small-town paper to go lunchless." I smiled as I rose to show I was joking. Mr. Ladd smiled back but I don't think he saw the humor of what I was saying.

"We'll have something to eat and then we'll head out to Little Goose so you can look over the house. How can you decide anything when you haven't even been to the island?" He was sounding cheerful again so I decided not to say anything blighting about my decision-making skills being excellent even without seeing the house. "Leave your bag here for now. I promise it will be safe. We have very little crime here."

We walked out of the office and he didn't lock the door. About forty feet up the street was the Great Goose Public House. The hour being advanced, we had the restaurant almost to ourselves. The interior was gloomy with soot-stained walls and small windows, but I thought it would look nice with a fire in the hearth and the candles lit.

"Is it sacrilege not to order lobster?" I asked, forgetting Mr. Ladd had no visible sense of humor. If Shakespeare's Beatrice was born to speak all mirth and no matter, then I was her opposite. But Mr. Ladd made me feel like a veritable comedian.

"Not at all—but you do like fish, don't you? It comes over fresh from Goose Haven daily. That is where most of the fishing boats are docked. They also have a lovely chowder house."

I do not especially like fish, but I didn't say it aloud since he seemed worried about pleasing me and dining options were limited. Scanning the menu I saw corn chowder in a bread bowl and opted for that.

There was a short wine list, but Mr. Ladd didn't even glance at it, so I contented myself with a cranberry soda. He requested coffee when our waitress came to the table. She studied me openly.

"Louisa, this is Theresa MacKay. Louisa and Jeb Parker run this place." Louisa Parker was forty going on sixty, her blonde hair fading into gray. Her eyes were pale blue but friendly enough even with their drooping lids. Her husband, who was working behind the bar, nodded but said nothing. He seemed a little older and not so much wrinkled as withered. His smile was charmingly puckish though.

"Please call me Tess," I said. Neither of us offered to shake but we smiled and nodded. "This is a lovely building. It's very old?"

"Ayuh, built in 1863," she said proudly.

We all smiled some more and Mr. Ladd ordered food with our drinks. I was a little surprised at him giving my order for me, but supposed it was just an old-fashioned courtesy that lived on in that small community.

I was given a local history lesson while I spooned my chowder, which was quite good. Mr. Ladd talked about the American Revolution, the fishing trade, the weather, the current inhabitants of Great Goose. Since I interview people for a living it was easy to absorb his lecture and nod at the right moments without ever betraying that parts of the verbal tour were not entirely fascinating.

He did not mention anything about my family or their place in local events.

Now I don't talk about my family either, but it seemed odd that given the Wendovers had been around for two or three centuries, he made no mention of them while recounting local lore. Finally he ran out of local wild birds and flowers to list and then apologized for monopolizing the conversation.

"That's alright. I don't actually know anything about the area or the Wendovers so it is all very interesting." Okay, I lied just a little. The recitation of local birds and flowers had gotten a bit tedious and I had stopped paying attention.

"Your grandmother never spoke of your family?" He was looking worried again.

"Almost never. She was very busy with the newspaper after my grandfather died and very … forward focused."

"This is the paper you now own?"

"Own and run. And write for." And printed, cut, and folded.

"Your hands are full then."

"Always. Fortunately I'm ambidextrous."

This got me another perfunctory smile. So he understood my jokes, he just didn't share the humor of them. Or maybe he didn't like being reminded that I had a life elsewhere and wouldn't be staying on the island, though why he should care so much remained a mystery.

After lunch, which he paid for and tipped a strict ten percent, he took me up to the market. It was in a corner building with a low ceiling. It was perhaps fifteen feet wide and maybe twenty long, about the size of a mini-mart, but it felt smaller and had less variety. There was no slushy machine or microwave food. Almost everything came in cans and they gave the impression of being dusty, though of course they weren't really. The shelves sagged slightly and there were footpaths worn into the floor.

Again, Harris Ladd placed my order after consulting me, explaining to the proprietress, Abigail Sibley, that I would need a few of the store's perishables. He recited the small list. Twice. This time I was feeling annoyed at his assumption that I would stay at the house long enough to need eggs and bread, but good sense came to my rescue before I spoke out loud. There probably weren't any inns on Great Goose and certainly not on Little Goose. If I wanted a place to lay my head that night, without returning to the mainland, it might have to be in Wendover House. And come morning, I would be wanting some breakfast.

Miss Sibley nodded, smiling blankly as she rang up my purchase on an antique register with a bent dollar sign. Reminded of Ladd's words, I began to hope that those small repairs to my house that the attorney had mentioned did not include the roof or broken windows.

After we collected my groceries from the ancient shopkeeper, who murmured something about being happy I was there, we went back to Mr. Ladd's office and picked up my shabby suitcase. As predicted, no one had stolen it.

We walked down to the empty docks to a small motor launch and Mr. Ladd handed me aboard. I have done some boating at home so managed to climb in with a bit of grace and stow my small bag under my seat while he cast off.

Little Goose was clearly visible from the waterfront and looked close enough to swim to, but the sea was not entirely calm and a quickly dipped finger assured me it was numbingly cold. Clearly I could rid myself of any notions about swimming in the frigid waters. That was okay. I had not packed a bathing suit.

The trip took only ten minutes and I enjoyed it thoroughly. The wind was brisk but the sun made it pleasant and I was getting very curious about the slanted island where my family had lived.

"Who lives here now?" I asked, raising my voice. This had also been absent from Ladd's luncheon lecture.

"There is a writer named Livingston. He writes some kind of spy books. He's from away." The attorney sounded disapproving. I wonder if it was a contempt of novels or for people who had the misfortune to be born elsewhere.

"Benjamin Livingston?" I asked, surprised and maybe just a little starstruck. He was one of my favorite novelists.

"Ayuh. He isn't terribly personable and always seems busy. Your great-grandfather never made him welcome, so don't expect him to be knocking on your door with a hot dish."

"Oh."

"Your other neighbor is Archibald Hicks, a retired marine biologist. He is from away too—Boston, I believe—and a bit of a recluse since his stroke. He lives with a nurse-housekeeper, Mary Cory. Mary's two brothers own one of the larger fishing vessels on Goose Haven. Nice girl. Very quiet though."

"Do people on the island own their own boats?"

"Most do, but the ferry comes on Tuesdays and Fridays. That is when groceries and mail are delivered. The ferry captain is Marcus Sibley. He's a quiet man, unless he gets a few drinks under the belt."

I was sensing a theme and it centered around "quiet."

"He is related to Miss Sibley?"

"Her brother." This surprised me.

15

"Is he … a younger brother?" Able to see and hear and recall three whole items at a time?

"Yes, a full decade younger and much healthier. And slightly more sensible." Mr. Ladd killed the engine and made the boat fast. He seemed to be pondering something and then after a moment, probably deciding that what he was about to share wasn't actually gossip, he said, "I know that Miss Sibley is rather elderly for the job of postmistress and shop clerk, but she has clung on because she is afraid to retire. Her father retired and died a day later."

Miss Sibley looked like she was barely "clinging" to more than her job, poor old barnacle. I nodded sympathetically though.

"My grandmother died in her office at the paper," I volunteered, taking his offered hand and allowing myself to be helped onto the dock. There were two other boats already there. One was a motorboat called the *Lubbock* and the other a tiny cabin cruiser called *Blue Ruin*. I smiled a little, wondering if the owner knew that blue ruin was an old name for rum. There was a sort of shed at the end of the jetty that perhaps served as a boathouse but it was empty.

"Did my great-grandfather have a boat?" I asked, thinking it would be convenient to have.

"He did but he sold it about five years back. He had a lot of trouble with it and once he almost drowned in a storm when the engine went out. He started believing he was a kind of Jonah and in the last years refused to leave the island at all."

Mr. Ladd insisted on carrying the groceries but I would not allow him to take my case. It didn't weigh that much and I was uncomfortable being treated as weak and witless, though that probably was not the intent of his gallant gesture.

The grass near the dock had been shorn, possibly by goats or sheep since it was uneven terrain. But there were flat places every few inches and we easily climbed through the rocky stubble without turning an ankle. I had read that some islanders imported grazing animals for the summer as a sort of natural weed-eater. Manure in turn attracted birds that ate the grubs in the manure and they in turn fertilized the grass with grub dropping that broke down quickly. This made for new and healthier plants. It was a natural cycle and helped prevent erosion. I just wondered how much the sheep liked riding in boats when it was time to move on to a new location. The thought of seasick ruminants made me shudder.

I'd best supply a little geography for you so you understand the layout. The island was a kind of triangle with blunted points. The whole thing tilted so two of the points were run right into the water. The remaining point was raised up about forty feet into the air. A fanciful person might think that a sea giant had grabbed one side of the island and jerked it down into the waves.

"That's Greyhome where the writer lives," Mr. Ladd said, jerking his head to the left. The house was not made of stone, but rather brick and wood. It was not large, but had two floors and a steeply pitched roof, probably necessary for shedding snow. "Beyond the copse of trees is May House. They were both built in the early nineteen hundreds. They brought in rental income until they were sold in the nineteen forties." The tone was trivializing of these architectural latecomers.

I could only see the uppermost dormers and chimneys of May House through the leathery foliage. This building was also made of wood that had been painted white. The black shutters were a somber note, but the house was attractive and seemed well maintained and I didn't understand the sneering attitude.

"Why are the houses here made of wood and not stone?" I asked.

"Building materials had to be brought in. The local rock is mainly shale and not good for quarrying. Wood was cheaper and easier to move."

"Ah."

Something large and gray streaked by us and I gasped before I realized what it was.

"It's just a cat," I said unnecessarily.

"Ayuh. Your cat, if you can catch him. The thing is half-feral. Kelvin was the only one who could get near him." Harris frowned at the bushes where the feline had disappeared.

"Kelvin?"

"Your great-grandfather, Kelvin Wendover."

"Oh." This information left me feeling disconcerted. Why hadn't I asked anything about the family on the trip over? For that matter why had I not asked for any details about who was behind "the Wendover estate" when I received the first letter? For some reason I was resistant to the idea that I actually had any kin, even dead ones. Maybe because they had always been characters in a fairytale. Or perhaps it was loyalty to my grandmother, but since she was also dead and I was there, it was time to ask some questions about the family I never knew. It wasn't like they could give me cooties or anything and, as the saying goes, one should carry rancor to the grave but no further. Whatever the old quarrel between Grandma and her father, it was time to let it go.

"There's a bit of legend about Wendover House that I feel I should mention," Mr. Ladd said. I had the feeling that he was reluctant to tell me the tale, but felt somehow compelled to share the information.

"What's that? Not ghosts I hope."

He frowned but didn't deny the possibility of ghosts.

"It's said that Abercrombie Wendover bought his property from one of the local tribes who had a sort of hermit medicine man that lived alone on the island, and that they put conditions on his taking up residence here before they would sell."

"Conditions or curses?" I asked jokingly when his face remained long.

"Well, a bit of both, I suppose. The legend has it that the three islands would be protected from invasion as long as there is a Wendover in residence on Little Goose. The owner can leave briefly, but a Wendover must reside here most of the time or on the next New Year's Eve the whole island will be drowned in vicious waves and pulled down into the ocean. It will destroy all ships in the water and drive the fish away forever. It is believed that the island is slanted because of the storm caused when the Indian hermit tried to leave."

I didn't say what I was thinking. I was too obstinately rational to believe in curses. Instead I asked, "Has this ever been tested by my family?"

"Sadly, yes. Abercrombie tried to leave the island but his boat, the Terminer, was overturned and he drowned in the freak storm that caused great damage on all the islands, destroying homes and many boats. His son was persuaded to stay on the island after that. They say he never left Little Goose at all. And his residency seemed to work since neither the British nor the French ever managed to set foot on the island during the wars, and any that tried to come were attacked by the sea and sunk. Having a Wendover on the island is considered a boon for the rest of us."

He was serious. The wind suddenly felt a whole lot colder and I considered the idea that I might be on an island with a crazy man.

"And here is the house," Mr. Ladd said, sounding awed and also, perhaps, just a bit nervous. "I trust you'll like it. It really is a historical gem."

Chapter 2

The house was white with green shutters, built in the Federal style, rectangular with no overhangs but a deeply recessed door where guests could stand out of the weather. The foundation was granite slab. It looked impressive perching there on its hill at the highest point of the island. It was ringed with stocks of bright purple fireweed, which I recognized because Grandma had grown it in her patio garden. There was also a kind of lawn area that would have been velvet in the spring but which had weeks ago turned into stiff blades that would poke through your clothes if you sat on it without a blanket. Perhaps once the yard had been manicured, but if so, there were no traces left of a formal garden. I found the wildness charming.

"You said Wendovers have been here since the eighteenth century?" I asked, not really up on my architectural styles but knowing the house was wrong for the era.

"The first house was partially burned during a bad lightning storm. It was when Abercrombie's son died."

"The one who stayed on the island?"

"Yes. A terrible tragedy. Only the daughter, who was away at the time, survived the fire. The name Wendover would have gone extinct but she was finally persuaded to return and her husband agreed to take the family name. It was said that he was…." Mr. Ladd frowned.

"Yes?"

"A smuggler and pirate and wanted by the law in New Hampshire. Of course, there's always been some smuggling hereabouts. Liquor mostly since it was outlawed for more than a century and certain men will always want what they shouldn't have." He sounded a bit prissy and I began to relax.

I couldn't help but notice the parallel with my grandmother's life. Maybe Wendover women made a habit of marrying disreputable men.

"That's colorful. How did they meet—the daughter and the pirate?"

"No one knows." The words were growing more repressive and I was betting the stories of that romance were pretty racy. I would have to look them up. Surely someone had written an account of this affair. It was too wonderful to ignore.

"Taking his wife's name was unusual though, wasn't it?"

"Very, but convenient when he was a wanted man. And perhaps he thought the Wendover name would protect him if he stayed on the island."

"Protect him from what?" I asked and was immediately sorry.

"From arrest and prosecution, of course." I didn't ask for clarification.

Mr. Ladd opened the door with a strange ceremonious air and then handed me the old-fashioned iron key that weighed about as much as a boat anchor. I would not be adding it to my key ring. We paused before entering, both of us waiting for some invitation I guess. Technically, I was the owner, so though it felt very odd I gestured the attorney inside.

I lost interest in the smuggler as soon as I stepped inside. It was a relief that the furnishings were not nautical. There were nine rooms in the main house, spacious, nicely appointed with antiques, or reproductions that looked so authentic I couldn't tell the difference. The place seemed a little overburdened with clocks, which would be noisy if they were all wound and ticking away at the same time, but that was the only off-note in an otherwise charming house. There were no obvious signs of damage to the walls or ceiling and no broken windows. The floors were level and the walls seemed square, suggesting the foundation was sound, so I hoped any repairs would be minor.

Every room had a fireplace. The openings were small and the fireboxes shallow. They had either a central tablet in the frieze with flanking columns or ornamental pilasters, or else lovely painted tiles with either nature scenes or indigenous animals on them. The hearths were clean but clearly the fireplaces were used and often. There were only oil lamps and candles on the various tables. It soon became apparent that the twenty-first century did not matter, or even exist, in Wendover House.

I was also struck by how tidy everything was. It would have been natural for some dust to have collected since my great-grandfather's death, but the house might have been cleaned the day before.

21

Of course, maybe it was cleaned the day before. If so, it was a thoughtful gesture from my great-grandfather's attorney.

"Plenty of coal and kindling wood," Mr. Ladd murmured as I peered into what really was a coal scuttle in what would probably be called the front parlor. I murmured something that sounded like agreement but was really closer to *you've got to be kidding*.

"Kitchen's this way. It is a little old fashioned but terribly charming." I thought the understatement was a sign of trepidation. I don't know many women who prefer charming to practical when it comes to kitchens.

A quick glance showed me that the original kitchen had been larger, but at some point the pantry had been installed along with windows, probably to provide ventilation. The few appliances were also new, replacing the old oven which had been built into the fireplace. It was also doubtful that the oak settle was original either, since this was probably the domain of servants and resting on the job would not have been encouraged.

Mr. Ladd probably expected me to be dismayed at the antique Magic Chef gas stove, but Grandma's first home—in Minnesota— had had a similar model and she had taught me to cook on it. On Sundays I would stand on a chair beside her and help make flapjacks. I was charmed. Which I told him while I looked in the bins and found flour, brown rice, and dried peas. Sugar was in a canister marked SUGAR on a battered work table made of what looked like pine. There was a copper kettle beside the stove, but everything else was tucked away into cupboards in labeled crocks. One said dried apples. I didn't look then, but checked later and it did indeed contained withered apples. There was a lovely crystal decanter in there too. A quick whiff was enough to identify the contents as whisky rather than sherry or brandy.

There was also a sack of dry cat food. I made a note to hunt for a bowl so I would know where to feed the cat. Experience with neighbors' pets had taught me that they were creatures of habit and apt to take exception to having their plans changed.

Appliances were limited, but there was an Edison Electric top monitor. It was an all steel refrigerator—again not unknown to me though an antique. Even with the radiator coil on top—which rather looked like a cookie jar—it was still shorter than I am. It was small but adequate for one or two people. It was just as well not to have anything larger because it ran off a generator, which was kept outside on the screened-in porch. The generator was not an antique and made very little noise when Mr. Ladd started it up. I suppressed a sigh. I should have guessed that there was no electricity on the island.

And no phone. But that was less annoying because I had a cell phone. No way to charge it, but I would be fine for the night.

"There are adapters that will work with the generator," Mr. Ladd said when he saw me checking for a signal. "Your great-grandfather had one but I don't know where it is. We'll get one for you. If you stay," he added when I looked at him with raised brows.

"Water?"

"From a well." He tucked my eggs and soda pop into the refrigerator. The bread he put into an old bread box. He seemed at ease in the kitchen, treating the room with familiarity.

"Hand pumped?" I asked, by then expecting the worst, though there was a sink and what I assumed was a faucet. It was copper and looked more like the swing arm from a standing lamp. In fact, it looked exactly like an inverted swing arm from a standing lamp, minus the light bulb.

"No. And there is a kind of water heater in the bathroom where there is a nice big tub—one of the old claw-foot kind. You just need to turn it on before you bathe if it's after dark. It is only a little noisy."

An old-fashioned tub—that meant cast iron which would suck the heat out of the bath water almost instantly. I was glad it was summer. Bathing in winter could be a penance.

"No shower?"

"No."

"Flushing toilets?"

"Of course!" He sounded offended. "There's a shared leach field used by all three houses."

"Where does that door lead?" It wasn't the pantry. I'd already seen it. It was the only door he hadn't opened and it was heavy and wrapped with large iron hinges.

23

"The basement. It's where the coal is stored, but I assure you that there is no need to go down there as the scuttles are filled. It is really more of a coal and root cellar and empty now."

"Don't worry. Basements hold few charms for me," I assured him, eyeing the attractive oaken settle on the opposite wall and wishing that I could sit down and have a cup of tea.

"There is something out back I want you to see." Mr. Ladd was beginning to smile and the easing of worry from his face made him look a lot more attractive.

We stepped out through a screened porch with a door that stuck and a workbench cluttered with gardening tools. We advanced about fifteen feet out into what had once been an herb and vegetable garden and he turned and looked up at the roof.

"Mind the plants. They're mostly slime now."

"What are those ... not solar panels?"

"Yes. But not for electricity. It heats water."

"Oh." I felt myself beginning to smile too as I looked at the zigzags of garden hose twisty-tied into wood frames. All at once I found that maybe I did want to know something about my great-grandpa.

"It's all chewing gum and bailing wire," Mr. Ladd warned. "Your great-grandfather was a bit of mad m—scientist. The gaumy thing works fine as long as it doesn't get too hot. If it gets too warm a valve sticks. It's there on the right where the ladder is." I looked through the rungs of a very old wooden ladder and there was some kind of box that had smudgy fingerprints all around it. "It's easy to pull out, but for heavensakes don't go up there while it's spraying water. Wait until dark or do it the next morning."

"Does it happen a lot?"

"Ayuh. It's what killed his garden. I came the day after he died and the scrid was stuck in. Boiling water was everywhere. Smelled like the worst vegetable soup ever made."

I had an urge to laugh and decided to go ahead and giggle.

"I guess it runs in the family. Grandma was always doing home repairs on her dentures and her typewriter, and my dad—" I stopped, remembering that it had been a home-design fuel injector that killed both him and my mom. "Well, I'll have to hope the day stays cool. I don't really want a baptism by boiling water."

"You'll be fine today. The heat has passed and it will be cooling off soon. You have a knack for coal fires if it turns cold enough? Mind it needs to be pretty darn cold or the chimney won't draw."

"Yes, I remember." I actually hadn't seen a coal fire since I was about eight, but there didn't seem to be much to it beyond feeding it coal as needed. It started the same as a wood fire with paper and kindling, though hardwood worked better because it burned hotter. Pinecones were excellent fire starters, but they put pitch up the chimney and made it more dangerous to use, so we had them only rarely.

Mr. Ladd—Harris—beamed happily. I had passed some kind of test.

"Most outlanders don't understand about these kinds of things. They don't appreciate that the islands are old, and the families too. Of course we get some from away every now and again but mostly we keep on with our own ways of thinking and doing and believing. But you'll do nicely here, I can tell."

"My grandmother was old fashioned," I said and let it go. No need to mention that she had used old appliances and had coal fires because she was poor for most of her adult life. Because she preferred to run away from home and marry a con man rather than speak to her family again. I changed the subject. "It's a shame about the garden. It looks like there used to be tomatoes. And that's basil. It would have made a nice salad."

"I suppose it's too late in the season to replant," Harris said regretfully. "But there is always next year."

I nodded but didn't comment. He had it fixed in his head that I was staying. I was only about ten percent persuaded. Of course, that was ten percent more than I had been when I got off the boat at Great Goose that morning.

"Mind that line of shrubs there," Harris instructed. "That is the end of the yard. There is a stack-stone wall beyond that is mostly sound, so there is no way to accidently fall unless you crawl out too far on the ledge. But go carefully anyway. Once in a while a bit of the cliff gives way after a storm."

"Don't worry. I have a touch of vertigo. I won't be crawling anywhere that's up in the air."

Feeling observed I looked over my shoulder and found myself the subject of a green-eyed stare. We had been followed. The gray cat with a crucifix of black fur on his chest and arms was sitting tall on what looked like the base for a statue.

"What did you say the cat's name was?" I asked.

Mr. Ladd hesitated.

"I believe he's called Kelvin."

"My great-grandfather named the cat after himself?"

"No. After his father. All the men in your family, since Abercrombie, have been called Kelvin. A fortune-teller told Abercrombie that the name would bring good fortune. Your great-grandfather was the ninth of that name."

There was no reason that this eccentricity should bother me, but it did. My family sounded extremely superstitious and even irrational.

"Here kitty-kitty. Here, Kelvin," I tried, kneeling down, but the cat shifted its gaze to Harris and laid back its ears. He came no closer.

Harris didn't try to cajole the cat. The antipathy was apparently mutual. Maybe he was a dog person.

"Well, if you are set, I should be going. You have my number if you need anything and I'll be back in the morning, say around nine?"

Again with the assuming. I hadn't agreed to stay the night, though I knew that I was going to do it. After all, I should spend one night in the old family home before I sold it. And I would sell it if a buyer could be found. I was seventy-five percent sure.

Chapter 3

I couldn't find the cat's bowl so set out a new one full of crunchies and one of water on the back porch. If the cat was hungry enough, he'd come and eat even in the wrong place.

On my own, I explored the house at leisure. It was excitingly old. I had never been in anything half so ancient. A place where so many people had died should have been filled with a heavy atmosphere, but it wasn't. Maybe because it had a cat and that made it feel still lived in.

In addition to the front parlor and kitchen on the ground floor, there was a dining room with a table that seated twelve, a library haunted by the smells of tobacco and leather and with a desk so massive it could withstand a hurricane, and a breakfast room that had probably once been a back parlor. Upstairs were four large bedrooms and two closer to closet size that had probably housed servants.

There was also a very narrow, very dark stair leading to an attic, but like the basement, I found this held little charm, especially when the sun began to set and the orange light picked out the dust and cobwebs. Though the pleasant odor of lumber lingered in the air, no cleaning had been done up there, not for a long while since there were no footprints in the thin layer of dust. So I closed the narrow door on the trunks and boxes, saving it for the morning. Or never.

There were oil lamps all through the house so I lit one from the parlor and carried it into the kitchen. Food choices were limited and I paused unhappily while I debated the merits of a can of stew or chicken noodle soup. Then I noticed another bin that proved to hold sprouting onions. There was dried basil and thyme and some barley, and lots and lots of dried split peas and several glass jars of pickled shallots and onion marmalade. I decided to make soup—without pickled shallots. There were no carrots or celery, but I found a can of new potatoes so I diced them up and threw them into the pot too. The soup was aromatic and made the house feel more inhabited and less like something on a historic tour. The can I rinsed and set aside; I would have to ask Harris how trash was handled. It probably went out on the ferry.

27

Around me, the house grew dark but also noisier as it settled in the cooling air which moved rowdily through the screened porch and shook the window frames when it found them. The door from the porch to the garden could be latched open, which I did, hoping the cat would shelter inside if it rained. A look at the near-empty bowls near an old Adirondack chair told me he had stopped by for a snack, so I hoped for the best.

I noticed the smell of ozone and wondered if we would have lightning. Other than worrying about the roof leaking, I had no real concerns about a storm. No one was predicting a hurricane and I'd experienced heavy rain before.

Leaving the pot to tend to the peas itself, I took my lamp upstairs and chose a room to sleep in. The beds were all made up and they were each rather handsome, but I liked the one at the front of the house with the maroon and gold striped walls best and set about making a fire in the tiny grate. For a while it seemed that the coal would defeat me, but eventually I got it lit and by then enough time had passed that I was able to eat.

It would have been ridiculous to set up the dining room for a lonesome bowl of soup, though I was tempted because the pretty but mismatched hutches that lined one wall had all kinds of china and silver in them. But I chose the modest breakfast room where I lit a second lamp and placed it in the center of the small maple table. I could see well enough with just the one kitchen light, but the gloom was beginning to bother me. I realized that at some point there was a turning of mood from cheerful bemusement at cooking my dinner on an antique stove to a slight nervousness at being alone in a strange place with the night closing in. It took me a while to recognize this feeling because usually I am not nervous about anything except paying the bills.

Partly the oppression was the intense dark pressing on the windows. Though I live in a small town, we have streetlights so the dark is never complete. There were no other lights that I could see beyond one in an upstairs room of May House.

It was full dark by the time I set the table and quite late for my dinner, so I ate without shillyshallying and washed up the dishes. Though tired and lulled by the rain that had begun to fall, I decided that sleep would not come quite yet and so stopped in the library to

28

select some reading material. The room, which had seemed very friendly in the daylight, now felt mysterious and perhaps even a little forbidding. It was also difficult to read titles by lamplight, so I gathered a few books at random to bring upstairs.

On the way through the parlor, I passed the spinet. I play piano and was looking forward to trying this older instrument, but not that night. It seemed wrong to make any noise once dark had fallen. I was too busy listening to strange sounds.

Not being as trusting as Harris, I locked the doors before I retired. It didn't strike me at the time that this was a sign of anxiety. It was simply habit.

The bedroom smelled faintly of coal, but this was not a bad thing. I settled my lamp on a table and got ready for bed. I thought about the bathtub and its strange water heater and decided that I would save that treat for morning.

I checked the sheets for spiders and silverfish, but everything was very clean and smelled faintly of lavender. I snuggled into the blankets after pummeling the old pillows into a bolster and then opened a book. The bed curtains I ignored since they might well be dusty and it was not that cold or drafty.

The first book I opened was a history of Maine, not my usual bedtime reading but I was interested enough to pursue it. The thought occurred that if I lived there I would probably do this every night. I might, in time, actually get bored with this routine. Though I tried to imagine that retiring with the sun and reading into the night would get tedious, I couldn't actually believe it. Most nights I worked late and worried. This was heaven.

* * *

My eyes opened, looking for danger before my conscious mind knew I was alarmed. There was a moment of disorientation before I realized that I was in my great-grandfather's colonial bed with only the light from my watch and the wind for company.

The fire I had lit before bed had burned down, leaving only the faint smell of soot. The moon was near full, but still obscured by clouds so there was no more than a faint glow to show me where the windows were.

29

I listened. I looked at the shades of black. Nothing was there. Nothing at all. Whatever I had thought I heard or felt, it wasn't real. My emotional alarm was probably just an aftereffect of long travel, a strange environment, and the suggestion from Harris Ladd that there was some kind of curse on the island. And maybe a ghost or two. Harris hadn't said anything about ghosts but silences also have emotional overtones and his had been fraught. I would bet anything that there were ghost stories about Wendover House. Didn't every old home have them?

These thoughts were all very rational and meant to be calming, but they didn't slow my thudding heart. Reason would not fix this problem.

A flash at the corner of my eye. I rolled my head. Light on the window—strobing, distant. The lighthouse of Goose Haven, I realized. Could that be what had awakened me?

Calm. I needed to be calm. I had a cell phone. I had a signal. I wasn't sure who to call in an emergency, but surely 9-1-1 would get me something. And there was Harris Ladd. But only if I was desperate. For some reason I did not want to appear ridiculous to him. Maybe because he already seemed inclined to treat me like I was slightly feebleminded. It was okay to respond to actual external stimuli but not imagination.

Enough. I would not spend the rest of the night cowering in bed, listening for clanking chains and werewolf howls. I would get up and assure myself that nothing was wrong and then go back to sleep. It took an act of will but I got out of the sheets. The phone gave me enough light to find the matches and light the lamp. I was careful with the glass shade but it still made what seemed to be a great deal of noise as I lifted it on and off. Why the hell weren't there flashlights on the end tables? Oil lamps were dangerous.

I didn't tiptoe but I walked softly. My socks were still on and they helped muffle my steps when I left the rug beside the bed. Down the stairs I went, cell phone in one hand and lamp in the other. I walked to one side of the steps, hoping it would minimize creaking. No one was there, of course. But still I wanted to be silent.

Step. Listen. Step. Listen. I stopped on the landing and held my breath. But there wasn't the smallest sound beyond the wind razoring through the garden and the last violent spatters of rain at the uncurtained window and the thudding of my heart. The house and I held our breaths and shuddered at the brief assault, but nothing else happened.

Ghosts, I thought again, but banished the word immediately. I was ashamed it even crossed my mind and the violence with which I rejected the possibility showed me how frightened I really was.

Down the steps I went on tiptoe until I reached the bottom. Then I smelled it. Felt it. Saw it in the lamp's brief wavering light. Fresh air, a small drought creeping over the floor and then up my body as it encountered the obstacle of my legs and decided to explore my trembling body.

It was coming from the kitchen.

It was harder to make the legs move after that, but move they did until I reached the doorway. Breath held, I lifted the lamp high and peered into the gloom. Nothing stirred inside the circle of light. I could hear the generator out on the porch laboring to keep my eggs cool. The smell of pea soup lingered in the air, first stronger then softer as it rotated through the room on the current that shouldn't be there. I advanced a single step so that I was completely inside the kitchen and began to turn slowly, lamp held high—stove, sink, work table, blackened chimney oven. Open basement door. I could see the edge of it beyond the fireplace chimney.

I almost screamed. Would have if terror hadn't frozen my breath. Fortunately, while in the thrall of terror, my intruder stepped into the pool of shivering light and I identified him.

His green eyes were wide and held fear equal to my own.

The cat. Kelvin. Somehow the cat had gotten into the basement and had come upstairs. The door had probably not been properly latched and being a large cat, he managed to get the heavy boards to open. That's probably what I had heard, the door banging against the chimney.

It was a cat. Not a ghost—a cat.

Finally I remembered that I needed to breathe.

"Here kitty. Here Kelvin." My voice was husky with residual fear. Setting the lamp and my phone on the table, I knelt down into the current of fresh air and put out a hand. "Good kitty. It's okay."

31

After a moment the cat came forward and rubbed his head briefly against my fingers. Then, his fear forgotten, he sauntered for the pantry. Exhaling softly, I followed. There was already a dish for crunchies out on the porch, but it was cold and wet and dark out there, and nothing would make me unlock the nice, thick door that was holding back the windy night. Instead I got out a new dish for kibble and a second one for water. They were Haviland china. I hoped my ancestors didn't start rolling in their graves at their debased use, but they were mine now, and perhaps the cat had more claim to them than anyone else did.

Kelvin gulped his food and I wondered how long he had gone without eating. I left him to his meal and, taking the lamp, went back to the basement door. The cold I felt from the dark mouth was not supernatural in origin. It was just a damp basement, but I closed the door firmly, making sure it latched. I looked for a lock but could find none.

Of course there wasn't one, I lectured myself. This was the only entrance and exit to a subterranean room that had no outside access. Locking it would be silly and even dangerous. There wasn't a lock on the kitchen or dining room door either and for the same reason.

Except the basement was creepy and should be locked. And how did I know there was no outside access? The cat had gotten in there somehow.

Okay. Reason it through. There wasn't any outside access—a human could use—because if there had been, the previous owners would have put a lock on the door. There was a lock on the front door and a lock on the back. Ergo there would be a lock here if there was some way into the house.

Still, I wasn't entirely comforted by this logic and there was absolutely no way that I was going down to the basement to search for a door while it was dark, so I went to the dining room and dragged out a heavy wooden chair. It wedged nicely under the latch.

This task complete, my adrenaline ebbed away. All at once exhausted, I turned back to the pantry to see if I could lure the cat up to the bedroom with me. This was a night for company.

Damn, I thought, retrieving the lamp. I had a cat. I'd meant to bring home some souvenirs of my trip—maybe a t-shirt or some postcards—but not an animal.

Should I bring him home? Could I bring him home? It was all feeling very complicated.

Chapter 4

I was up with the sun, never having really fallen asleep again, in spite of Kelvin snoring on the blankets beside me.

Unable to lay there any longer, I watched the sun fight free of the water and the few remaining clouds. My first and foremost desire was for a hot bath, so I sat down with the detailed written instructions left in the tub and figured out how to use the strange water heater. It seemed to work like a giant electric tea kettle. Like a tea kettle, I submerged no part of my body in the water while it was heating.

My bath wasn't deep, but it was warm enough and I felt more able to face life once I had washed away the last traces of the night's fear sweat.

The face that looked back at me from the mirror though was not one I had seen before. Of course it was my face, but it seemed to have grown thinner, paler just overnight, and I had hollows under my eyes. I told myself it was just a lack of sleep and that old mirrors were sometimes imperfect, distorting.

Though I was still feeling very henhearted, I went downstairs, started some oatmeal and dried apples, and then went to look at the basement. If the cat could get in then other animals could too. I didn't know what lived on the island besides birds, but I was pretty sure I didn't want the local animal kingdom's representatives living in the basement.

Kelvin followed me to the kitchen but was happy to stay in the pantry and eat his breakfast so I was on my own for exploring.

I stood by the chimney listening and thought I heard a sly scratching. Kelvin appeared immediately and stared fixedly, gaze aimed upward into the flu.

Birds, I thought, with a welcome blast of common sense. Someone had built a nest in the chimney. It would need to be cleaned before winter.

The basement waited while I dithered. It still seemed sinister to me, but what was sleep deprivation and what was valid judgment I couldn't really say. Some people are procrastinators, but I'm not. Especially if there is something unpleasant that needs doing. Unable to delay any longer, I went to the door and listened.

Dragging the chair aside, I opened the door and peered down the stairs that disappeared in the smelly gloom. Even with the morning sun filling up the room, I was going to need a light to see anything downstairs. There had to be something better than the oil lamps and I looked around hopefully.

My eyes were delayed a moment at the porch's screen door, which I could see through the window. It had remained open during the night so that the cat would have shelter. Unfortunately, the more energetic gusts of wind had brought rain inside to swell and stain the plank floor. That wasn't good. The boards would need to be sealed before winter because even storm windows wouldn't keep all the weather out. I made a note to mention this to Harris.

I went back to the kitchen and began opening drawers under the work table, all the while keeping half an eye and both my ears fixed on the dark opening to the basement. Finally I found a flashlight. The casing was cracked and the beam was weak but it was better than the oil lamp, so I made do.

Damp earth, dust, the nascent smell of decay. I hate that basement scent. The cat's tracks were on the stairs, but so were others. Probably my great-grandfather's, I realized, and shivered. The mud had dried so there was no knowing when they had been left—possibly a long time ago, I told myself, but….

My parents were not imaginative people and if Grandma Mac was, I never saw any evidence of it, so I had not been raised to fear the dark or the things that might inhabit it. But I disliked this particular darkness and could all too easily imagine things lurking in it—ghosts and skeletons and ferocious rats.

Still, it seemed better to go down the stairs in daylight and find out what was there than to wait for it to creep up some night and surprise me in bed.

Wondering if I was being as stupid as all the women in the monster movies who go down to the basement when they know they shouldn't, I pressed on until I was on the last stair and then stopped. I played the light around the room, examining it before I stepped onto the floor.

The room was empty, just as Harris had said, not one skeleton or rat in sight. The floor was dirt and stone, the yard-sized sheets of paving rocks laid in a circular pattern that I felt I should recognize but couldn't place. All I could think of was Greece and Crete and stories of labyrinths, though I didn't think the pattern was quite right for that.

Three walls were covered in shelves and a plywood bin was heaped with coal. The fourth wall had cupboard doors made of some kind of heavy wood. One at a time I pulled them open, revealing old crockery, antique tools like a carpet beater, a damaged storm shutter, some ancient canned goods so old that their contents were no longer identifiable, and one locked door that wouldn't budge no matter how hard I pulled on the handle.

By then more piqued then terrified, I went back upstairs and started searching the kitchen for a key. Eventually I found one, but either it was the wrong one or the doors were jammed, perhaps the wood warped by the damp, because I couldn't get the last set of doors open.

Defeated, I stepped back to regroup.

In any event, the cat hadn't come in that way, so the contents of an old cupboard didn't really matter. It was just curiosity that drove me to want the door open—just to be sure about the lack of rats and bones. But that wouldn't be happening right away so I needed to be patient and not pick up the rusty old ax and beat the door into kindling.

"Okay, so what now?" I asked myself aloud. "How did the cat get in?"

I didn't feel any air currents around me to suggest a likely opening hidden in one of the other walls, but the storm had passed so perhaps that lack of air current was natural. Short of removing every cobwebbed item from every shelf and looking for a cat-sized opening in the walls behind the clutter, I wasn't going to find where Kelvin had gained access. Was it really worth the effort?

Before I could decide how ambitious I was feeling, there came a pounding at the front door. It was faint but persistent. I glanced at my watch and realized that it was probably Harris and that I was dusty and that my oatmeal might very well be cold.

"Good morning," I said, opening the door and then blinking at the stranger on the doorstep.

He was a tall man, middle aged, pale, rectangular of face, and at the moment unsmiling. I recognized him from his author photos and felt a small flutter in my stomach.

"Good morning," he said politely but with less enthusiasm than I had shown. "I saw a light moving around last night and thought perhaps I should come by to see who was in the house."

"Tess MacKay," I said, smiling and offering my hand. "I've inherited the house from my great-grandfather."

The sandy brows flew up but he took my hand and shook it once. I hoped he wouldn't notice that it was still a little smudgy.

"So Ladd finally found someone. That will upset some people on Goose Haven, though the fishermen will be happy enough. The betting pool at the chowder house is running heavily in favor of no heir ever being found."

"And you are Benjamin Livingston of Greyhome, the writer *from away*."

The face relaxed just a trifle and I was pleased. Everyone here seemed so serious. I thought my sense of humor had atrophied in the last few years, but these guys made me look like a jokester.

"*Away* being Philadelphia."

"I'm from really *away*. I live in Minnesota."

"But you are a Wendover—that makes you a local. You even look like a Wendover. It's rather uncanny." This was news to me. I was tall and dark haired like my grandmother, but I wasn't aware that this was a family "look." "Has Ladd explained about how this is a wonderful place to live and that you must take up residency at once?"

"Yes. I just fear that maybe our definitions of wonderful may vary slightly."

"Good luck convincing him of that. He very badly wants a Wendover in this house. A lot of the locals are very superstitious, you know. They think of Wendovers as being weather charms. Silly, of course, but with most of them I doubt you could knock that notion loose with a ballpeen hammer."

"Hm. Which one is the ballpeen? I can never remember and I want to be sure I have the right one on hand."

A twinkle, a definite twinkle. I decided that I liked him. Why hadn't he and my great-grandfather gotten along?

37

"Would you care to come in for some breakfast? I have just made some oatmeal. It has cinnamon and apples so it should be edible."

I am not sure if my offer would have been accepted, but at that moment Harris Ladd crested the hill. My stare alerted my guest to the visitor and after glancing over his shoulder, he declined politely.

"Morning, Ladd," Benjamin said, now barely amiable but making it obvious that the cold shoulder was for Harris and not me. I got a friendlier nod though no smile, and then he was gone down the same path without another word.

"Good morning, Tess. You passed a pleasant night?" Harris was dressed casually in chinos and windbreaker but somehow still managed to convey an old-fashioned formality.

"Not entirely."

He began to frown.

"The storm worried you?"

"No. The cat decided to let himself into the basement and then into the house around two this morning."

"The cat was in the basement?" Now he was frowning in earnest. "But how can this be?"

"I guess there is a cat door somewhere. I couldn't find it though. It may take some hunting. The shelves down there are packed with junk." My oatmeal was probably glue but I was still hungry so again made my offer of breakfast. "I've made some apple oatmeal, would you care to join me?"

Harris hesitated but his jowls quivered in a telling manner, so I pressed him.

"Is not the laborer worthy of his hire?" I asked, and earned an actual smile. Men were unbending right and left, before you knew it they would be breaking out in fits of jocularity and smiling hard enough to show some teeth. "And if it tastes ghastly you don't have to eat it."

"I should be glad to join you." He stepped inside. "Will I be laboring today? Have you decided to remain a while longer, or is my job to take you to the ferry?"

"I'm staying. Just for a few days though." I was sixty percent sure that this was true. "But I will need to get a few things if I am to spend another night here."

"What do you need? Shall I take you to Great Goose or will you need the mainland?" He sounded enthused. Maybe Benjamin was right about the locals being really superstitious. The idea was weird and amusing.

"Well, I need some milk," I said, walking to the stove and lifting the lid on the cast-iron pot. For a mercy the oatmeal was still warm and smelled wonderful. "I will also need more kibble. Kelvin is eating me out of house and home."

At the reminder of my feline guest's presence in the house I looked about for the cat, but he had disappeared. I decided that after his enormous meals he might be feeling the call of nature and opened the back door that led onto the porch and then into the back garden. The lock was noisy as I turned it and I knew that Harris probably wondered at my having used it.

"But mostly I want some flashlights—preferably the crank kind that don't need batteries—and a lock for the basement door."

"Certainly, there should be flashlights, but do you think a lock is necessary?"

"I do. Somehow the cat got the door open and I don't really want the rest of the island wildlife following him inside if he does it again." This was a secondary consideration. Mostly I just really didn't like the basement and wanted the door locked at all times. That little voice inside doesn't speak up real often but I have learned to listen to it.

"That would certainly be bothersome. I believe that there are rats and rabbits," Harris agreed, accepting the offered bowl. "I'm glad to see you've mastered the stove."

"I have even conquered the immersion heater in the bathroom. I suppose my last trial will be the solar panels but I am hoping to be spared for a while longer."

Again Harris smiled.

"Let's eat in the breakfast room," I suggested, not wanting him to see that one of the dining room chairs was missing and again being used to hold the basement door closed.

We sat down at the small table and dug in.

"This is lovely," Harris said. "I haven't had oatmeal since my wife died."

"I'm sorry," I answered and was. "When did she pass?"

"It's been four years now. It was a boating accident," he said. The comment did not invite follow-up and I took the hint.

"Will I need to go to the mainland for supplies?" I asked.

"I believe a lock and your other items, of course, may be had in Goose Haven. It is about a twenty minute ride, if you are inclined? The sea is fairly calm today so the trip would be pleasant."

"Water doesn't bother me," I said. "We have a lot of lakes in Minnesota. Of course, I wouldn't go out in a storm, but you needn't worry about me coming down with seasickness or anything just because of choppy water."

"Good. Then we can go whenever you like. I have left the day open and am entirely at your disposal. Let's see if we can't make you more comfortable here. We don't want you to hurry away."

Livingston was definitely right. Harris really did want me to stay on Little Goose.

Chapter 5

The clouds were like wooly lambs gamboling in the brightest of blue skies. The water sparkled, the grass was vivid green. No one, not even an inveterate alarmist—which I am not—could be afraid on such a morning. Almost I forgot the apprehension of the night before.

Almost.

"Remember not to whistle," I said to Harris as he helped me into the motorboat, recalling one of the sailors' superstitions I had read about while researching a piece for the paper on Friday the 13th and other things that bring bad luck.

Harris looked startled.

"I beg your pardon."

"You don't want to raise a gale," I explained.

"Oh. The local fishermen do believe in some strange things, but I think that one has gone out of fashion even with the older folks like my parents."

"So, I can't make my hair curly by rubbing rum on my head?" I asked as he cast off.

"I fear not."

"My grandma believed in an odd one. She said that you should never rock an empty rocking chair because it would lead to someone's death."

"Ah. Here they believe that rocking an empty chair will call a ghost," Harris answered. He was still smiling but his lips looked strained. I guess rum on the head was silly but empty rocking chairs were not.

"Maybe you should sing to the sea," he suggested. "Music soothes the waves. A harp is best, I understand, but we must be practical."

"Glad it doesn't take a piano," I joked, but not feeling entirely comfortable anymore. I had never been around someone who was so very superstitious. It seemed odd that he could be so educated and yet so irrational. I supposed that it was all in how one had been raised.

Since I am not rude and couldn't think of anything else to say about soothing the sea, it seemed a good time to turn the subject to things more comfortable.

"I hear that the chowder house is excellent. Mr. Livingston mentioned it." In the context of gambling, not for its food. "I'm curious to see it."

"We can eat lunch there, if you like," Harris said cheerfully. He had to raise his voice as a small flock of seagulls had decided to fly by and shout at us. None were rude enough to do anything worse. I got the feeling that he liked being out on the water.

"And how does Goose Haven differ from Great Goose? Is it just the fishing vessels and the chowder house that elevate it?" I asked.

"The lighthouse lends a certain distinction. You may purchase a postcard of it if you wish to amaze your friends."

Harris was teasing me. He certainly had unbent from the day before. I would have to ply him with oatmeal more often.

"I certainly must do so. Souvenirs are also expected by coworkers when anyone travels."

"There are commemorative t-shirts and snow globes."

"Perfect." We were silent for a bit, watching the water and the birds, then I recalled a favorite quote from a seventh grade English teacher. "They change their skies but not their souls who travel across the seas."

"That is by Horace, yes?" Harris asked. "For many that may be so, but I think that often beginning a new life can lift burdens of the spirit."

My spirits were feeling less burdened, that was for sure. Stay or leave—and I was still fifty percent sure I would leave—the money I had inherited from my great-grandfather would be a big help. The leafy green dollars the newspaper ate were not growing on any local trees. The whole economy had been sprayed with weed killer and we were just another of the wilting businesses. Our subscribers had been flaking away like the paint on the office door, and though I tried cost-saving measures, we were already so lean we were bone and there was no support from the staff, who selfishly continued to like eating. Sometimes I thought I was the

42

only one at the paper who noticed what was happening. Certainly I was the only one who cared.

Would anyone want to buy the paper if I decided to stay in Maine? What about Glory Peace nee Braverman. The new hubby was springing for a facelift. Would he want a newspaper too? Glory did like to be in charge of things and maybe she would be better at the job. I have a tradition of procrastination that annoys her. It's self-defense though. Do the setup too early and someone will die, or a baby will come ahead of schedule, or there will be a surprise engagement to mess up the layout. But procrastination can lead to a second office tradition: panic. It doesn't happen every week or even month, but at least four times a year the printer breaks down and I have to scramble to find a loaner.

"Are you feeling okay?" Harris asked solicitously.

I sighed as I heard my thoughts encroaching on the lovely day. My true-blue and loyal was beginning to fade. In my heart of hearts, I didn't want to keep on with Grandma's dream. The paper just wasn't what I wanted to be enslaved to.

"Definitely," I said, forcing the frown away. "What kind of fish live in these waters?"

We arrived at a busy wharf that smelled of bluefin tuna and black sea bass and all the other species Harris had named. I tried not to wrinkle my nose at the odor. Most of the boats were out plying their trade, but there were still several people moving about in the dockside shacks, mending nets and coiling ropes and doing things I couldn't guess at. They nodded politely at Harris and me, but none spoke to us until Harris stopped beside two very old men sitting in an open-sided shed. They perched on stools with a barrel between them. They were playing checkers, about a third of which had been replaced with bottle tops. Both looked like they came from central casting.

"Morning, Ladd," said the one with silver hair and bloodhound eyes.

"Good morning, Jonas. Morning, Saul. This is Tess MacKay. She is Kelvin Wendover's great-granddaughter."

Now both the silver-haired and white-haired man were nodding and smiling. There was curiosity but no surprise. Word of my arrival had spread.

43

I smiled and nodded back. There was no direct verbal greeting however. Apparently Harris would be speaking for me again today. I guess I was to remain a woman of mystery.

"What ails Amos?" Harris asked, nudging an animal that was at least part Great Dane that was laying at Saul's feet. The dog sighed but didn't look up.

Hoping I wasn't being presumptuous, I knelt and stroked his head. His brindled coat was very shiny.

"He's glum. The last batch of beer went bad—tasted like it had been washed out of his own kennel. Dog wouldn't even drink it. Had to pour it out. Happened only wunst afore. We're waiting for more hops to arrive."

The dog thumped his tail, either enjoying being petted or else recognizing the word "beer."

Knowing I might well be reprimanded for speaking out of turn, I volunteered a bit of beer lore I'd researched for Oktoberfest.

"They used to use dandelion and horehound instead of hops for bitters," I said. "In Germany."

"Likely that's so, them being Germans," Jonas agreed.

"Don't that beat all?" Saul asked, smiling benevolently.

I nodded again and stood up. Once again, trivia had come through for me. Many people dismiss collections of small facts as irrelevant, but I have often found "silly rubbish" useful as icebreakers in social situations.

Encouraged by their forbearance, I ventured to ask a more personal question.

"So did either of you bet against Harris finding an heir?"

There was a moment of silence and then both men began to laugh. I glanced at Harris. He wasn't laughing but his expression was rueful.

"I suppose that busybody Livingston told you about the betting pool. I hope that you don't think less of us for it."

"Yes, he told me. And I am not at all surprised about the pool. It's exactly the sort of thing that happens in all small towns everywhere. Probably even in big ones. I expect a cut though from whoever wins," I joked.

That made both old men laugh harder.

"Best stop at Mike's," Saul finally advised. "He's got your winnings. Missy here sounds impatient, Ladd. Best calm her before she raises a gale."

I lifted a brow at Harris.

"Your winnings?"

"Well, I had to have the courage of my convictions," he explained with feigned dignity. "I couldn't leave the challenge unanswered, and I was quite certain that I would find someone eventually."

"Good to have a Wendover back on the island," the more loquacious Saul said. "Happens we'll have a good winter now."

I shook my head as we turned away, but didn't correct the assumption that I was staying.

"Did you have a cutoff date for finding someone?" I asked Harris.

"Yes. New Year's Eve."

I recalled the legend he had told me about the island sinking into the ocean if a Wendover wasn't in residence. I had an inborn prejudice about certain beliefs and the propagation thereof. But I know that I am closed-minded about certain subjects and try to keep my skepticism and disapproval to myself.

"Well, I don't suppose there would be much point in searching if all there was to inherit was a drowned island."

"Quite," he said, but wasn't looking amused. Maybe I wasn't hiding my contempt for superstition well enough.

Harris took my arm and pulled me against the wall as a white Westie jingled by. He was followed by an elderly scarecrow walking purposefully toward the dock but turning at the last moment to enter a building flying the state flag. The Westie's coat was glossy but no match for the perfect silver hair on the man, which looked like it had just been buffed and polished at the factory. Harris got a short glare as he went in the door. I received a shorter glance that was no friendlier.

"It's the Reverend Ezekiel Burke," Harris whispered. "Retired. He's from Salem."

I nodded, not sure what to say. That was a puritanical face that launched a thousand bonfires. Clearly there was a story here, but I was getting to know Harris and he wasn't going to tell me anything unless I pushed it. This was getting tiring.

"I'm sure that he has excellent manners when he's had time to shine them up."

"Don't count on it," Harris muttered. "He thinks we're all godless heathens clinging to our pagan, lawless ways. He especially disliked your great-grandfather."

Did he think that? I wondered if he were right. Certainly people seemed rather given to strange beliefs and I noticed several of the buildings sported "witch balls." They were really just old glass balls used to float fishnets, but many people thought that hanging them over the windows and doors would keep out ill wishes and bad luck. Still, that didn't mean people drank blood out of skulls or drowned virgins on May Day.

"I suppose, this being New England, that there has to be one religious eccentric in town. Though I think it is rather rude of him to just assume I'm a godless heathen. Just because I apparently look like a Wendover doesn't mean anything. I might be a lovely widowed person who teaches Sunday school to orphans and gives all my money to the poor."

The tension left Harris's body.

"It's very rude and you are a lovely person. Don't let his prejudice give you a distaste of the town. You will be very welcome."

We started walking again.

"The pagans weren't really godless or lawless, you know. He must not be much of a historian if that's what he believes."

I think Harris laughed, but it was silent and over very quickly.

"If you ever choose to tell him so, I would like to be there to hear it. A rebuke from a Wendover might make him faint from fear and spleen."

Mike's Chowder House was doing a brisk business. It was a very masculine place. The only soft touch was an apologetically small vase of dried flowers at the end of the bar, and given its placement, behind what looked like a pickle barrel, I had the feeling it was left out due more to forgetfulness than sentimentality toward the donor.

It was too early to eat again but I enjoyed meeting the owner and was carelessly introduced to Everett and Bryson Sands, the local law. Though I suspect it surprised them when I reached out to shake hands in a businesslike manner, they took my proffered fingers and pumped them once. I kept my grip kind of limp and ladylike.

Someone called to Harris and he excused himself and went to collect his winnings. No one seemed surprised about the betting, though the one officer scowled a little as he stared after Harris.

"So which of you is Bryson and which is Everett?" I asked.

It turned out that Everett was the younger of the brothers, the thinner, the more bleached, and the more uptight. His smile was there at the proper moments but he didn't mean a single millimeter of it, and his hands were callused and scarred. I was betting he did some fishing. Bryson had hair the color of peanut butter and was more slow moving and slow talking. I wasn't sure if this was because of personality, massive size, or a lack of ambition concerning his career. The slightly enlarged midriff and slouched posture didn't mean anything one way or the other. I'd been a reporter—albeit a small-town one—for long enough to know better than to judge someone by their appearance even if—*especially if*—they conformed to a stereotype by, for instance, eating donuts and sipping coffee at ten in the morning. He might very well be someone who talked slow but thought fast.

Bryson offered me a lazy smile and a direct gaze, as though guessing he was the subject of my thoughts and finding my assessment amusing. I adore men with brains and I let myself smile back.

"I won't judge if you don't judge," I said softly and got a laugh. Everett looked blank.

"Best offer I've had all day," Bryson answered. "You should try the blueberry donuts before you go."

"I will."

Harris rejoined us and handed over his ill-gotten gains, asking Everett to give the money to his sister who ran some kind of benevolent fund for injured fishermen. After some polite goodbyes where I found myself saying that the brothers should feel free to visit anytime they came to the island, Harris and I headed to a sort of antiques and hardware store, clearly marked by the wheelbarrow full of books parked on the wooden walk.

"I think Bryson took a shine to you. That's nice because Kelvin was not always his favorite person," Harris said. He wasn't prying, but I knew he wondered what had amused the older policeman.

"I told him I wouldn't judge him for eating donuts if he didn't judge me for being *from away*." And female. And a Wendover, I guessed, if he hadn't liked my relative.

Harris nodded.

"Bryson is a shrewd man. Some people miss that because of his casual demeanor."

"Looks are deceiving sometimes," I agreed, thinking how much I apparently looked like a Wendover and how little that meant to me though it seemed significant to others. "And Everett?"

Harris forgot his dignity and shrugged.

"Everett is more formal. Less relaxed. Some people call him judge-and-jury Sands. Bryson keeps him from the tourists. Oddly enough, Everett and Kelvin got along fine. I never understood why, but he came to visit Little Goose every few weeks."

Harris opened the Mickle's Emporium door for me and I stepped inside the shadowy shop of old things and new things which looked old. The creaking floors were hand-pegged like they were in Wendover House, though these boards were far more battered and they had never enjoyed a coat of wax.

Morris Mickle, the proprietor, was introduced and after a nod, Harris set about explaining what I wanted. Morris had a lovely soft voice but he used it very little. He gave the impression of being slightly moth-eaten, a taxidermy left forgotten on some shelf. I wondered if this was by design.

After some searching in a shallow bin, he decided that he did not have a keyed lock for the basement door, but he had a heavy bolt that would work as well. He had also just gotten in a stock of crank lantern-flashlights and crank radios. Harris complimented him on his acumen and he looked pleased.

I got one radio and three flashlights and an adapter for my cell phone charger. That seemed like overkill if I was leaving in a few days, but I had been thinking it over and decided that I wanted time to go through the attic and look for family photos and maybe a few keepsakes to bring home. There was no reason to get back to Minnesota right away, so why rush? And besides, there could be antique treasures in those trunks and crates.

Morris reached under the counter and pulled out a green fishing float which he wrapped in newspaper and added to my bag.

"A house warming gift to keep you safe—though of course you've no need of it," he said with a shy smile and a guilty glance at Harris.

"Thank you," I said. "I will hang it over the basement door. I think I have boggles down there."

Morris blinked but didn't say anything.

I was prepared to pay with a credit card as my purchases were loaded into a mesh bag, but Harris told Morris to send the bill to his office and he'd see it was paid at the end of the month.

"Everyone runs a tab. It's just easier," Harris explained as we left. "And the estate should pay for these expenses for now. Probate will take about two weeks more. Then the money will be yours free and clear, but for now, don't take on the burden of debt."

"I'm impressed that it is only two weeks," I said.

"We are not a populated county. There aren't that many people pressing claims ahead of you, and I started the ball rolling the moment I found you."

The next stop was the grocer. Morris Mickle's parents owned it. They were introduced as Mr. and Mrs. Mickle. They were straight out of *American Gothic*, missing only the pitchfork, and this time I didn't offer to shake hands or attempt any off-topic conversation. Frivolity would not be welcome by the dour pair.

Harris did not protest my purchase of a large bag of cat kibble. He probably saw all of this shopping as a sign that I was thinking of staying permanently. I was about forty percent sure he was wrong, but there was no point in trying to deny that I was enjoying myself that morning and maybe the fantasy of living there—in the summer—crossed my mind a time or two.

Again, Harris set me up with a tab and suggested that I might like to schedule regular deliveries of perishables and fuel by ferry on Fridays, including the large bag of kibble, unless I needed it immediately. Feeling slightly cornered, but also amused by his maneuvering, I agreed to have a pint of milk and a half dozen eggs delivered every Friday. Additional items for an order could be phoned in on Thursday, Mrs. Mickle explained, and they would be added to the grocery box. Accounts were settled at the end of the month, unless the last day happened to fall on a Sunday. Then Monday was fine.

I also picked up some Gouda cheese, two postcards which I addressed to my coworkers and mailed immediately, and a Mrs. Crumpert's blueberry pie.

By then it was after noon and I was feeling peckish. It may have scandalized Mike, but I ordered a hamburger instead of clam chowder with a donut for dessert. More pea soup was waiting for me at dinner and I wanted some large animal protein.

Harris and I chatted comfortably as we dined. I asked about Kelvin and he told me about some of my great-grandfather's wilder inventions and ongoing feud with a local fisherman called Dandy Dawes who liked to set his bug pots (lobster traps) too close to the island. Kelvin considered everything within a hundred feet of shore to be his own private fishing ground and warned everyone else away. In the interest of peace, the Sands brothers had backed him up and Dawes was terrorizing lobsters elsewhere.

Though Harris didn't come out and say anything directly, I got the feeling that Kelvin had been a law unto himself, a bit tyrannical even, and I wondered how far his eccentricities had gone. There had to be some reason for my grandmother's willful amnesia about her early life, and an even better reason than any I had heard for her to run away and stay away until she died. I thought this also explained where my grandmother's towering stubbornness had come from.

There was something else odd about the situation though. My great-grandfather had not been an idle man. He had invented a lot of things and tinkered with the house. But I got the impression that he had not exactly been a roll-up-the-sleeves and work from nine to five kind of man even in his youth. He wasn't a fisherman or a lawyer or a carpenter. He hadn't owned a store or painted houses.

In fact it didn't sound like anyone in the family—since the pirate—had toiled and survived by the sweat of their brow. What had they done with their time? Where had the family money come from? How had they survived?

The contrast to my grandmother's life—to my own life—couldn't have been stronger.

Chapter 6

Harris insisted that I see the lighthouse, which was open to all visitors in spite of being overseen by the Canadian Coast Guard. It was very narrow and claustrophobic inside and I declined to go all the way to the top, knowing it would provoke my vertigo.

The clouds were gathering as we headed back for Little Goose and we had to work our way through the returning fishing boats. Everyone stared and nodded at me and most waved at Harris, though no one shouted any kind of introduction or greeting. Maybe bellowing at ladies was considered bad form.

The air as we neared Little Goose held the expectation of rain and I began looking east with regularity as the clouds thickened and roiled. Harris said this was normal weather for summer and that I would have to watch the sunset, which would be spectacular. I took comfort in his calm demeanor.

At my request we circled the island before docking. The sun was in the wrong place to have a great view of the house, which was mostly just a silhouette, but I got to see more of the island itself. The cliff that fell away from my backyard was dark shale with pockets of soil which had probably washed down from the garden and gotten caught in the fractured stone. Small, scruffy plants were growing in the cracks and it seemed that seabirds were also nesting there.

At one point I thought that I heard a booming echo that can mean a sea cave, but I couldn't see anything in the growing shadows and Harris disclaimed any knowledge of Little Goose's topography or geology, though he admitted that caves were common to the area.

I might have asked Harris to get closer to where I heard the sound, but the wind had picked up and the water was choppy enough to make me uncomfortable with the large rocks peeking between the shadowy waves. I was used to boating on lakes, not in the sea which rises up and down with the tides. I'd never seen stones look so savage and the changing tide made the boat harder to control. Searching for caves was an activity for a calm morning when the sun would light the cliff face and surrounding sea.

Though my day on Great Goose had been lovely, I admit that my nervousness returned as we approached the house, and I found myself asking Harris if he would like to stay to dinner when he finished installing the bolt on the basement door. He accepted and seemed to enjoy my variation of egg fried rice, but we had to eat quickly so he could beat the dark and the storm back to Great Goose.

I felt almost sad waving Harris goodbye, though I wasted no time shutting out the dark and wind. Like the night before, I closed and locked the doors before retiring upstairs. Deciding that I wanted just a bit more of Mrs. Crumpert's utterly delicious pie, I helped myself to another slice and then put out kibble for Kelvin, who had appeared on the back porch the moment we had the house to ourselves. I let him in, accepting the scolding for having gone off and left him all day with nothing more than an enormous bowl of crunchies and water for company. There seemed no point in explaining that he could have come in while Harris was there. The cat just didn't like my attorney.

I had to clean out the fireplace before I could lay another fire. Something about the smell of the ash made me melancholy. Coal made sense on the island, but if I stayed, I would want to have wood brought in. Wood reminded me of bonfires and camping and happy wholesome things. Coal was industrial and lonely.

* * *

I woke when Kelvin jumped from the bed and landed on the naked floor. He went to the bedroom door and mewled softly, patting at the wood with an enormous paw.

Feeling slightly more confident about getting up in the dark now that I had a lock on the basement door, I reached for my flashlight—all fully cranked and ready to brighten the night—and turned it on.

Kelvin's eyes glowed at me. He meowed demandingly.

"I'll get you a litter box tomorrow," I told him. But that didn't solve the problem of his wanting out right then.

Kelvin meowed insistently and since I also needed the bathroom, I gave in. Sighing pointedly, I pulled on my robe, wishing I had something warmer to wear. The nights were chillier than I had expected.

My door opened silently, though the house was far from quiet that night. There was wind in the eaves and rain hurled at the leaded windows. In the distance, the sea grumbled. Timbers creaked and groaned. But that was okay. These were outside noises and normal old house sounds.

And there was a lock on the basement door. It would keep out anyone and anything. At least anything earthly in nature and that was all I was worried about. Because there were no ghosts.

"Don't go there," I whispered. "Don't even think about it."

Kelvin frisked down the stairs and disappeared into the dark. I did not frisk. I clung to the bannister and listened carefully as I descended. Animal eyes watched me—foxes and hounds, dead pheasants, one large black and white cow, an owl. And cats. Lots of cats that looked like Kelvin. I hadn't noticed the paintings before. Perhaps in daylight one wasn't aware of all the staring eyes. Or that none of the eyes on the wall were human.

Nothing stirred, no sound and no movement, but I did feel the chill as it began to inch up my legs. Even in summer with much longer days in which to heat the house, nylon was not protection enough from the night air.

Or fear.

I turned my light on the front door. No cat. He wasn't at the back door either. It did not surprise me to find Kelvin scratching at the basement door and meowing impatiently. I had no intention of opening it, even with my witch ball hanging overhead, but I went to the panels and laid an ear against them. I could hear nothing through the thick wood.

Because there was nothing to hear.

"Come on, Kelvin. We aren't chasing mice in the middle of the night and if you have a box down there, well, it's just too bad. If you need out, it will have to be the back door."

But Kelvin didn't want the porch or the yard. He remained at the basement door, staring and sometimes scratching while I tried to coax him away with kissing noises and leg pats.

"No way," I said for a last time and turned back for the stairs. "I'm going back to bed. You can do what you want."

After a moment, a sulking Kelvin followed me to the stairs. He stalked ahead of me when we reached the bedroom and jumped onto the bed. He gave me a hard look and lay down. I had to move him from his chosen spot right in the center of the bed and this earned me a cold shoulder when I tried to pet him. I was sorry for it, but there was absolutely no way that I was opening the basement door at night.

I fell asleep thinking that it was odd that there were so many pictures of animals in the house, but none of any people. Where were my ancestors? Had none of them had their portraits painted? If not, why not?

Chapter 7

I woke with the sun, having spent the rest of the night in troubling dreams about sinking ships and faceless smugglers hauling barrels of rum from ship to ship while storms raged. I had forgotten to draw my drapes and the bedroom was dazzling with morning light.

Though feeling very purposeful and resolved on some research, or at the very least finding some photos or paintings of my mysterious ancestors, I made myself fix some eggs and sip some tinned orange juice for breakfast.

A careful tour of the living areas discovered no portraits in any room. I hadn't seen any in the basement either, so that left the attic as a possible repository of art.

The air was stale at the top of the house and I stepped carefully so as to not stir up the dust on the attic floor as I went hunting for photographs or paintings of the family I had never known. Though Hollywood would have us believe that there are as many monsters in attics as in basements, I found the smell of dust to be much less upsetting than damp earth and felt not the slightest stirring of unease.

My first family find was not a photo album, but rather a painting, a seascape which had been leaned against the wall just inside the door. It was realistic but rather dark, perhaps simply aged or maybe grimed with soot from hanging over a smoky fireplace. I could make out that I was looking at Little Goose, Great Goose, and Goose Haven, though there was no lighthouse and the only building was on Little Goose. There was also a ship sinking in the stormy sea, torn open on Goose Haven's rocky shore. A lone figure was on the deck. Carrying the canvas close to the tiny window I could make out the ship's name. It was the Terminer. Abercrombie's ship.

If anything should have given me the shivers it was that painting, but I felt not a tremor. Not happy subject matter, of course. I could understand why it had been relegated to the attic. Had Kelvin done it when he thought he was becoming a "Jonah"? It wasn't pretty, but still, it was my first look at something and someone connected to me, however distantly, and I decided to

56

bring it downstairs and hang it again. Later I would ask Harris about getting it cleaned.

I turned next to the trunks and crates that lined the wall, making the room feel smaller than it should. The first chest opened with a blast of camphor. It held musty textile treasures, each wrapped in aging fabric. There was a fur caplet that must once have been white but was now very yellow and balding. I rather liked the black Astrakhan coat, but it was too large and a bit tatty for wearing in public. And anyway, it would be hard to wear it and not think of the newborn sheep that had died to make it.

Though careful while unwrapping the yellowed muslin, there was still a bit of an explosion as I opened the last article in the trunk. Inside the old linen, there was a molting muff made of disintegrating bird feathers which started me sneezing but provided Kelvin with some entertainment as he chased the strays around the room. He was getting dusty, but I figured if there were any mice, Kelvin would keep them in hiding so I didn't shut him out of the room while I worked.

Someone had been busy. I found a box with hundreds of crocheted doilies done in all colors not found in the rainbow. Old as they were, the dyes remained garish. Too nice to throw away, but too ugly to use, they had been banished to the attic.

Some of these things should be thrown away, but it didn't seem my place to do it. Not yet anyway. The clothes weren't harming anything; they could stay until either someone else took care of it, or I felt less presumptuous about attending to the task myself.

There was a bride's chest suffering from water damage that was filled with yellowed sheet music. A quick look showed me that it wasn't for spinet but rather for harp. I had a quick glance around, but none of the shrouded shapes that lined the walls resembled a harp and I knew there was none downstairs. When had it gone from the house and who had been its owner? The era was about right for Great-grandpa Kelvin's wife, but might also have belonged to my grandma. Grandma Mac had never shown any musical inclination though, so I doubted it was hers.

Curious now, I began pulling away tarps from the furniture along the wall. I found a cradle and some elaborately carved wooden chairs that needed refinishing. There were eleven of them, which seemed odd until I looked closer and saw that the varnish on the remaining chairs had been scorched and even blistered by heat. The twelfth chair must have burned beyond saving. I couldn't repress a small shiver, thinking of Harris's words about the fire that killed Abercrombie Wendover's son. Not liking that I was feeling fey, I still backed off from the burned furniture and left the damaged chairs alone.

There was a wardrobe too, a great blocky thing carved with wheat and fruit that was probably once attractive but one side of it also showed blistering of the varnish. The finish could be restored, which was why it was upstairs, I supposed, but I doubted that I would be the one to do it.

It was placed inconveniently, right in the middle of the wall, as high as a door and deep enough I had to step around it as I dragged out the various boxes for examination. I thought about moving it aside, but it was filled with taxidermies, moth-eaten animal masks and mounted fish, and I was afraid it would be too heavy to move unless I emptied it first. Since I had no desire to touch the rotting things, I decided that the wardrobe would stay in place.

The second crate opened reluctantly but was worth the effort. It was lined in cedar and filled with heavy damask that was embroidered over in silken thread. Each panel was made of pieced fabric, the cloth only being about two feet wide, though the seams were cleverly hidden. The workmanship was exquisite, the miniature flowers and birds so clear that I believed that I could pick them up. The style was a sort of tree of life, but along the bottom there were ocean waves filled with fish and boats.

A bit of lifting and shaking revealed that they were bed curtains and not window drapes. The cloth was remarkably well preserved, the colors strong, and the only fading was in part of one lining. The patch of lighter cloth looked a little like a handprint. I searched for initials, hoping the embroiderer had left some token, but could see none.

I wondered why they had been so hastily packed away. Carrying them into the light where the colors exploded at the touch of the sun, I began to picture them hanging around my bed.

Kelvin sneezed and then mewed. He retreated to the door, feathers forgotten, as he glared at me, correctly placing blame for his sinus distress.

"Bless you," I said and then froze in place. The brain had made one of those intuitive leaps. Sneezing—disease—death. The curtains had probably been put away when someone died and the surviving family had not been able to endure the reminder that their owner was lost.

I hadn't a shred of proof that this was true, but my gut said I was right.

Part of me hesitated, instinctively recoiling from the deeply ingrained notion of the contagion of death, that bad luck—or germs—might cling to a dead person's possessions and kill me too. A part of me wanted to shove them back in their crate and go scrub my body. The rest of me realized that had there been any question of contagion from a "catching disease" that the drapes would have been burned and not just stored in the attic.

Gathering up the fabric so it didn't drag on the dusty floor, I carried them and the painting downstairs. Though the curtains did not appear especially dusty, I decided to fetch up the carpet beater I had found in the basement and give them a good beating before hanging them around my bed. I wasn't afraid of ancient germs, but I saw no point in making myself miserable with the ancient dust that had the cat sneezing.

Kelvin and I went out into the garden. I found what I assumed was a line used for drying stored inside a washtub with a wringer. Looking in the logical place, I found two eye-hooks and hung the line.

There was a bad moment when I tripped over something and found a rotting head half-buried in compost, but Kelvin pounced on the staring eye. Digging with his paws, he soon revealed part of a marble statue, a broken casualty, beheaded fairly recently. Somehow it had ended up disintegrating under the remains of the dead garden killed by the erupting solar panels. The cat dug some more and I was able to see the marble body. It was chipped in several places and I began to wonder if my great-grandfather might not have been using it for target practice.

"Thanks, Kelvin," I said, wiping off my hands, which were suddenly sweaty. "But don't you think you are dirty enough?"

The cat swished away, sneering at my concerns over cleanliness.

I tossed the drapes over the thick cord and then made myself head for the basement for the carpet beater I'd seen there. I'd never used one before but the principle seemed obvious.

Kelvin, not ready for his midmorning nap, came with me. I turned on my kitchen flashlight, feeling cheered by the manmade light and the cat's calm presence. Having watched Kelvin with Harris, I was pretty sure that he would be showing hackle if we were not alone. Cats were also supposed to be sensitive to spirits and otherworldly things.

Though feeling much braver for having manmade light, I did not dawdle on the narrow stairs. I recalled where the carpet beater was and hurried directly to the cupboard. It was only as I turned back to the staircase that I again noticed the muddy footprints that had dried on the floor. Were there more of them than the day before?

"No. I can just see them better now that I have a stronger flashlight."

Kelvin mewed an agreement and after a bit of rubbing and sniffing on the bottom step, he led the way back up the stairs and into the sunlight. I wasted no time getting back to the yard, but made sure that the basement door was bolted shut behind me.

I beat the curtains for a while, encouraged by the clouds of dust I was getting off of them. Kelvin kept his distance, sneezing and hissing at them when the breeze made them flap his way. After a time I decided that I too had had enough dust and exercise and took a break. The wind could do the rest of the work for me.

I collapsed on the porch steps, turning my face up to the sun and enjoying the breeze as it dried the probably gray sweat on my face. As I rested, my breath calming, again I heard the distant booming that might mean a sea cave. It was a lonely and even scary sound. I didn't like the idea of the sea eating away at the island. And Harris had said that sometimes the cliff would give way after a storm. Given enough time, the house itself would fall into the ocean.

Deciding that I had had about enough alone time for the morning, I thought that I would clean up and then go and ask Ben Livingston if he knew anything about caves on the island and perhaps invite him to lunch. There had to be something decent I could make for a company meal.

Back in the kitchen I washed my hands and face and had the rest of my tinned juice to drink. Beating curtains is hard work. My respect for my ancestors grew with every primitive labor I performed.

I didn't lock my door. The key was a monster to cart around and I felt no need for security during the day. The garden was empty of everything but flowers and carpenter bees. The rain water hadn't puddled so everything was fresh rather than soggy.

The way to Greyhome was made clear by a fork in the path which was lined with columbine and butterfly weed. There was also some kind of rambling rose growing over the door, pouring out its honey scent into the air, but before I got close enough to steal a blossom I was summoned away by a horn down by the docks.

"I wonder who...."

I climbed onto a convenient boulder and looked toward the wharf. It was Friday, I realized, and the ferry had arrived. Kelvin would be happy to see more crunchies and I would have a fresh supply of eggs. Feeling a little bit excited, I hopped down and hurried for the dock.

Ben and a dark-haired woman I assumed was Mary Cory were already down at the wharf and receiving boxes from the crew of two. I wondered if the ferry always came at this time and then realized that it depended on the tide. The water would need to be fairly deep to accommodate the boat. Everyone probably kept tidal charts right by their calendars. I likely had one on the desk in the library and just hadn't noticed.

"Good morning, Tess," Ben said as I joined them. His tone was neutral but I felt the only vaguely remembered pull of something that was close to attraction. The sensation surprised me and I wondered if it were mutual. It very rarely was, at least in my experience. "Let me introduce you to our other neighbor, Mary Cory."

The woman nodded. Her bleak eyes, puddles of gray in bloodshot whites that looked slightly jaundiced, studied me for a second and then dropped. I didn't think it was modesty. I wondered if it was a hangover.

"Hello," I said but didn't offer my hand. Women did not seem to shake hands here and she had a small box of groceries in her arms which she seemed to be paying a lot of attention to.

"Hello," she finally muttered back. I looked at Ben and raised a brow.

He shrugged. Maybe Mary just didn't like *away* people.

"As it happens, I was just on my way to see you, Ben."

"Yes?"

"I wondered if you knew anything about a sea cave on the far side of the island. I keep hearing this kind of echoing booming when I'm out back and I wondered if there might be a cave there. I asked Harris but he says he's never heard of one."

"I don't know either," he said slowly. "No one has ever mentioned one to me, but I suppose there might be. Lots of islands around here have them."

"I've heard tell of there being one," Mary volunteered, still not meeting my eye. Her voice was flat. "It's supposed to go in apiece. I never looked for it though. Kelvin wasn't big on people exploring his property. And those sea caves flood at high tide. Plenty of away folks have drowned in them. It's best to just stay away."

"Oh, that's too bad. I've never seen one." I couldn't help but feel that her words were overly discouraging. I wasn't sure why I was so excited about the idea of a sea cave, unless it was from reading about the local smugglers and pirates.

The man I assumed was Captain Sibley dropped a large sack of cat food at my feet and thrust a small box of groceries into my arms.

"Ma'am," he said, jerking his head in the slightest of nods. His cap was pulled down almost over his eyes. He didn't smile and spent his time gazing past me. I began to wonder if I shouldn't have checked a mirror before coming out. Maybe I was a lot dirtier than I realized and my filth was embarrassing people.

"Tess, this is Cap'n Thomas Sibley."

"How do you do?" I asked politely. "Thank you for bringing out the cat food."

"Ayuh," he said, nodding again and then hurrying away. It occurred to me that he was afraid of something. Was it me? Or just the island? Or, I thought as I turned at the sound of a strident meow, was it the cat? Some people had strange phobias, but Kelvin was just sitting on a rock, looking as unthreatening as a flower. Surely it couldn't be that.

"You weren't planning on looking for that cave alone, were you?" Ben asked, handing me a small box with dried cereal and a bottle of milk and picking up the enormous sack of cat food and hoisting it over a broad shoulder. He might be a bit pale from being indoors but he wasn't weak.

"No. I would need a boat anyway. The cliff face is too sheer to climb down." I put a box under either arm so I was more balanced. Cardboard boxes didn't seem ideal carriers to me, especially if it was raining, though I supposed the market probably had tons to spare and they would stack better on the ferry.

We started up the trail. Mary went in front since we couldn't walk three abreast. Kelvin followed behind Ben, perhaps keeping an eye on his dinner.

"That's true. Can you recall when you've heard the booming? Was it high or low tide?"

"Near high tide," I said, thinking back. "I could hear it just before the ferry came today but it was getting fainter by the minute."

"Would you mind if I came back with you and had a listen?" he asked. "You've made me a bit curious. I've been doing some research about local smugglers and pirates and I would love to see a cave, if one exists."

"Since you have the cat's food, definitely not," I said with a smile. Mary was outdistancing us and she didn't look back. I had the feeling that we weren't going to become the best of friends.

"Is she cold to everyone?" I asked Ben. "Or just newcomers?"

"She keeps company with Everett Sands sometimes, but mostly she is a loner. Don't take it to heart."

"I won't." But I did kind of. "So could I interest you in a slice of Mrs. Crumpert's blueberry pie first? I am suddenly starving."

"You got one yesterday? I missed out this week. She only bakes pies on Thursdays and people snap them up right away."

"Well, I have one. Half of one. But I'll share."

"Then I don't mind being the beast of burden for your cat."

"Thank you for doing this. I am relieved it's not raining. This path would be a pain."

"Me too, though the ferry usually delays if there is a gale."

"Speaking of gales, did you hear about my ancestor who adopted the Wendover name because he was wanted for piracy and smuggling in New Hampshire?"

"As a matter of fact, yes. I've read about it. Didn't talk to Kelvin about it since he was usually so touchy about his ancestors. Kelvin maintained that the reprobate reformed, but I don't think your fly-by-night relative gave up his evil ways after he married. The locals certainly suspected him of smuggling."

"Really? That's kind of ... fun. But stupid, I guess, if everyone knows what you're doing."

"There was a lot of money in liquor in a dry state. A lot of men ran rum to make ends meet. It happened in the best families. And anyway, there would not have been that much disapproval from the locals. The Wendovers were important people in the community. I have a feeling that their little eccentricities were tolerated."

"Hm. I guess everyone has colorful relatives. I found a creepy painting up in the attic. You know the story of how Abercrombie Wendover drowned? It's a painting of that. I'm thinking of hanging it in the library."

"You can actually tell it's the Terminer?" he asked excitedly.

"Yes, you can read it on the sinking ship. I am kind of hoping this doesn't mean I have ghosts at the house." I tried to sound like this was a humorous idea, but really I wasn't amused. "I also hope that I can find some portraits up in the attic. It seems very odd to have nothing but pictures of animals hanging on the walls."

Ben cleared his throat.

"I don't want to shove my oar in, but have you considered having electricity run up to the house? I don't know how you could stand it there when the storms are at their worst. It would have anyone thinking about ghosts."

I stopped in my tracks and Kelvin began twining around my ankles, urging me to keep up with the kibble.

"What?"

"I said why not run electricity up to the house?"

Never mind that I might not be staying on the island, I heard myself say, "I can do that? I mean, the lines have already been brought to the island?"

"Of course. You don't think the rest of us would live here without power, do you? Kelvin was just too damn stubborn to have the house wired." Realizing I had halted, Ben stopped too and turned back impatiently. "I thought I had him convinced, but the electrician said the minute he told Kelvin he needed to install a fuse box in the basement the old bastard—er, pardon my language—the old man threw him out. He wouldn't hear of it, though the electrician explained that the wires have to go underground in a pipe and that means the easiest place to enter the house is through the basement."

Goosebumps covered my arms. I'd have paid them more heed but anger was flushing my cheeks.

"Why the hell didn't Harris mention this? I mean I've been managing with the weird solar panels and oil lamps, but this has not been a convenient stay."

Ben shrugged. He didn't smile but I could tell he was amused by my wrath. I tried to recall if Harris had told me there was no electricity on the island, or just none at the house. Surely he wouldn't have lied—not when I could and probably would find out about there being power on the island.

"I guess he's honoring Kelvin's wishes. Ladd is a traditionalist and very loyal to your great-grandfather."

"Kelvin is dead. It's my wishes that count now." I started walking again. "Okay, maybe he didn't say anything because I haven't committed to staying. He did say some repairs were needed before the house could be sold but we didn't go into details."

"Maybe so. I know historical preservationists would prefer to leave the place as is, but I can't help but think that the cottage would sell better with a few modern conveniences. Not everyone is as intrepid as you and Kelvin. Ladd should know this."

I snorted. Harris did know this and probably just didn't want me to sell the house. Well, he would be hearing from me shortly. Though mentally planning the conversation, I was also thinking about something else Ben had said. *I thought I had him convinced, but the electrician said the minute he told Kelvin he needed to install a fuse box in the basement the old bastard—er, pardon my language—the old man threw him out.*

Why? What the hell was in that basement that Kelvin didn't want disturbed? And why wouldn't Harris want me to have electricity at the house?

Because it might make it easy to sell it and then I could leave? Did he really believe that I had to stay or the island would be pulled down into the sea?

Chapter 8

We went out to the yard to have a listen for the cave, but the booming was gone. Ben admired the drapes I'd been beating and helped me carry them in and hang the bed curtains in my room. I was glad he was there because it would have taken me a while to figure out how to remove the rods which were cleverly fitted into the finials.

We had some pie and then Ben gave me the name of the electrician who had worked on his house. We were, as my grandmother would have said, getting on like a house afire. Ben asked if he might go through my library one day and I said he was welcome.

I called Harris as soon as Ben left. Remembering Grandma's other adage about honey catching more flies than vinegar, I buried my annoyance and kept everything upbeat, expressing my enthusiasm for modern light bulbs over quaint oil lamps. Harris didn't try to dissuade me, but I sensed a lack of zeal and I could hear him pacing up and down his narrow office as we talked. He did point out the expense. I countered with the argument of convenience. I didn't mention how much a buyer would like having electricity, just kept it to a discussion of how much easier it would be for me to live on the island if I had a computer and coffee maker. Though I hated playing games, I did it, and soon Harris was agreeing to my ideas and even offered to call the electrician for me.

I wandered around the house after I hung up, feeling almost dreamy and making some tentative plans. Electricity could make the difference between staying and leaving, I thought, touching the furniture and even playing a few bars of *Silent Night* on the spinet. I was trying to picture the room with a Christmas tree and red candles, but before I could get them lit or the mistletoe hung, I heard the distinctive crash of a bag of kibble being knocked over in the pantry. A moment later Kelvin came running by the door and then thundered up the stairs as if chased by devils. I laughed once he was out of earshot.

The house felt very alive to me that afternoon, very welcoming. I couldn't believe that it was all mine and that it came without strings—at least no emotional ones since I hadn't known Kelvin and didn't mourn him. And Harris hadn't mentioned any legal strings either. Even probate would be through in a few more days. There was only the half-baked legend about there needing to be a Wendover in the house to appease the storm gods and I wasn't buying into that obligation.

This sense of belonging was a new experience. I had to admit that the idea of leaving the house, even temporarily, now that I had laid eyes and hands upon it was increasingly less appealing. I felt like I really belonged there. This was the home I never had. This was where the changeling fitted in. I was grateful to Kelvin. And Harris. And the gift came without any shadow of grief to darken the moment.

Haven't you noticed that usually, when someone dies, their home immediately feels empty and the people visiting for the funeral and cleanup are intruders in the vacated space? Maybe it's because many of the deceased's possessions are suddenly ownerless and worthless. After all, who wants an old hairbrush or beat-up sneakers or photo albums of other dead people that no one recognizes anymore? Their owner conferred their worth and meaning and now they are gone. Most everyone already has their own ratty sofas and wobbly dining room tables. The dead person's beloved stuff is fit for nothing but a thrift shop, and stripped of its personal things, the house is just a shell, built to be generic, able to house anyone.

But that wasn't the case at Wendover House. These possessions, these heirlooms, had never been ownerless or neglected. The house was never uninhabited. When one Wendover died, another took their place. Changing fashion was not considered. One did not discard the hand-carved grandfather clock in the parlor or the fine tapestries in the library because a new owner had different tastes. The furnishings were immutable, existing when their owners were dust.

Certainly I would not bring anything of mine here to pollute the space.

Except clothes and some family pictures.

And a television and DVD player. And my computer.

So, okay, maybe the office would change a little. And my bedroom. I would not sully the public rooms with a television, but I would allow my bedroom to be degraded because I really like watching old movies in bed.

Imagining my computer in my new library office, I wandered back into the book room. My eyes fell on the painting I had left leaning against the wall after Ben and I had examined it.

I needed a hammer and a nail. I had seen some in the kitchen.

After hanging the grim picture behind the desk in the library where it was in a place of honor but where I wouldn't be forced to stare at it all the time, I opened the central drawer and began looking for a tidal chart. The drawer didn't open more than about six inches before it caught on something.

I jerked it a couple of times, but without real force since I didn't want to damage anything. Though my mission was pure enough, I still felt presumptuous going through a desk that didn't belong to me. Oh, legally it was mine, but morally? Unlike the other objects, the desk felt like it still belonged to Kelvin Wendover.

Sighing, I pulled out a bent tablet covered in crabbed writing and peered into the gap to see what was sticking. Amid the pens and paperclips and other normal desk detritus there was a gun. A nine millimeter, black, fairly new and very ugly. The barrel was pointed right at me.

I didn't touch it.

A dueling pistol or a derringer, or even a blunderbuss or fowling piece, I would have accepted without question since they went with the antique theme of the house. But this modern thing was out of place in this elegant and aged desk. And why the heck had my great-grandfather wanted it anyway? Did he have cause for worry about either of his neighbors? Or had he gotten senile and perhaps paranoid? Was that why Bryson Sands had not been friendly?

I closed the drawer carefully, wanting nothing to do with that handgun or the questions it raised.

Feeling unnerved and wishing to reclaim my upbeat mood, I began dusting the library shelves, straightening books and reading titles as I arranged them. My favorite find was an Ansonia clock, about seventeen inches high and made of brass. It was so elegant that it looked like it belonged on a fireplace in Versailles. I hadn't wound any of the clocks in the house, but if I found the key, this one would be put to use.

There were some blank spots on the shelves and the books that remained were in some disorder. Kelvin had obviously not been fanatical about his shelving. Amid the expected volumes about maritime law and state history, I found a book on witchcraft which had fallen behind a stack of almanacs. Normally this was something that would interest me, but for the time being I left it alone. It was getting late and I didn't want to read anything disturbing before bed. The day had been lovely and I didn't want to jinx it.

On a high shelf I found the family Bible. It was a brute of a book and the leather cover was cracking along the spine. I set it on the desk and opened it carefully, reading through the names— Kelvin, Kelvin, more Kelvin—then Grandma. The entries stopped there.

Because she had run away, married a man and changed her name instead of him changing his to Wendover.

And she had daughters instead of Kelvins.

And the eldest daughter had had a daughter.

Now I was back on the island but there was no Wendover in Wendover House. Was I supposed to find some man to marry who would change his name and start having baby Kelvins again? Was this what Harris—and maybe others—secretly expected? The idea was disturbing but it made a kind of sense. If you were crazy enough to believe legends and had missed the whole women's movement.

I found a folded paper tucked in the back of the Bible. It wasn't signed, and the handwriting was slightly larger and more rounded than what I was used to, but I was pretty sure that the note had been penned by my grandmother.

I can't do it. Let the ocean have it. Daddy, you might be willing but I will not stay.

This had to be a reference to the legend about there needing to be a Wendover in the house on New Year's Eve. Had my grandmother—that strict rationalist who objected to fairytales—actually believed this nonsense? Or had she used this excuse because it was something Kelvin would understand? After all, it would be hard in that day and age to admit that you were running off with a traveling salesman because you were in love, especially if your parent was not entirely rational.

The room darkened as a cloud arranged itself in front of the sun. Suddenly the house felt less charming and more like a honey trap that had drawn me in with the lure of beauty. I put the note back in the Bible and returned it to the shelf.

Though it was early, I decided to eat cereal for an early dinner, using up my milk as quickly as I could. The eggs I would use for breakfast and lunch in some form or other so I could turn off the refrigerator. The generator was quiet as engines go, but it seemed silly to run it for a mostly empty refrigerator, especially with gas being as expensive as it was. And I would be able to hear better without its low throb in the background.

Though I hated the idea, I decided that I needed to go back down to the basement and have another look around before dark. The cat had gotten in there somehow and maybe that existing opening was one that the electrician could use to bring in the wires. And also seal up when he was done.

Whether I stayed on the island or put the house on the market, it needed to be electrified. It wouldn't be inexpensive because so much of the island was rock, so I needed to find savings where I could.

Kelvin, done sulking upstairs, didn't mind going down to the basement and I half hoped that he would lead me to his hidden exit, but he just climbed up on the highest shelf and began grooming. Scowling at his uncooperative attitude, I set the lantern on the floor and began removing items from the shelves, dusting them half-heartedly with some kitchen rags before replacing them. The old canning jars were wooly with cobwebs and dust and would need boiling before they could be used again.

My phone rang halfway through the empty canning jars, the forgotten sound scaring me nearly to death.

71

"Hello?" I gasped when I had fumbled it out of my pocket.

"Hello? Tess, are you there?"

"Jack? Is that you? Wait. I'm in the basement. Give me a sec to get upstairs." I hurried up the steps but the cat didn't follow. I had half an urge to bolt the door anyway, but decided to start retraining myself. The basement door being open that first night had made me into a scaredy-cat. The door could stay ajar until the cat reappeared. That would prove that I was a rational adult.

"Jack? Is this better?"

"Much. Look, I just read the paper and saw your announcement. You're in Maine?"

"Yes, on an island called Little Goose."

"Should I offer condolences? Was it someone close? I didn't know you had any family left."

"My great-grandfather died. I didn't know that there was anyone left in Maine either, but it turns out there was. Kelvin Wendover. He's left me the house and some other investments."

There was a pause.

"Are you coming back?" Jack asked bluntly.

"I don't know. I would come back to pack of course. And to sell the paper, if I can find a buyer. Maybe Glory will want it," I added hopefully. "The thing is that I'm slowly realizing that there just isn't much else to come back to."

Jack exhaled and I hoped he wasn't insulted. Our breaking up had been as much his choice as mine and he had already started looking for a second job.

"I'm rather glad to hear this," he confessed. "I've been dreading telling you, but I've had an offer from *The Trib* and I'm going to take it. It's better money and, well, a chance for more interesting work. Also, it would get me away from Kathy."

"That's great," I said, and tried hard to mean it. This changed the balance of my own equation. Without Jack, the paper would be almost impossible to run. "How's the leg? Healing up?"

Another pause as Jack accepted that I was changing the subject.

"Yep. Another two weeks and I'll be good to go. How are you doing? What are you doing? Do you like living on an island?"

"I ... I don't know. I have a rather interesting neighbor. You'll be jealous when I tell you."

"Who?" he demanded, beginning to relax as we got away from personal things.

"Benjamin Livingston."

"No! I heard he was living in Maine, but what are the chances of him being next door?"

"It's true. He has one of the three houses on the island."

"Three houses? Okay, I want the full story. Are you really living in the back of beyond, or is this a joke?"

So I took a deep breath and started telling him.

"Well, first off, I've inherited a cat and there's no electricity in the house. There is also a curse on the island...."

I talked for half an hour straight and then my phone began beeping, complaining of a tired battery. When I hung up I felt cleansed, but also a little uneasy that I had transferred my angst onto Jack. He had needed to be reassured several times that there was nothing truly sinister about Harris or the island. And there wasn't. I was just more imaginative than I had ever realized.

I went to the basement door and called the cat. When Kelvin failed to appear, I fetched his food bowl and rattled the crunchies. That worked much better. Kelvin and I returned to the kitchen and began considering further food options. I started with washing my grimed hands. The solar panels really did provide hot water as long as the sun was out, but it had wheeled into the west hours ago and the water was only tepid.

My spirit might be cleared by my talk with Jack, but my clothes were a mess. I was going to have to do some laundry. There was the washtub on the back porch, but I could have hot water if I used the bathtub. I wondered if everything would dry overnight if I started laundering at once. Or right after a light but late after-dinner snack.

"I hate doing laundry, Kelvin. At least by hand. I wish I had packed more."

Then I thought of the bedroom upstairs, the blue one with the white counterpane and gilded bedposts. The room I had chosen to sleep in had been empty of clothing, but the blue one had had some clothes in the wardrobe. I hadn't paid attention to what kind of clothes but my impression was that the previous inhabitant had been of the female gender.

"I wonder...."

Kelvin followed me upstairs and entered the pale blue room without hesitation. Perhaps he felt at home because there was a painting of a similar looking cat on the wall.

There was enough sun to see by without lamplight as long as I held the garments near the window. As I feared, most were inappropriate, silks and delicate linens, arranged so tidily that I could almost see my grandmother folding them. Everything reeked of mothballs, but I found a pair of high-waisted slacks in camel wool and a cashmere sweater in a shade of mustard that Grandma Mac had always favored. There was also a pair of jeans in a style my grandmother called dungarees.

"Kelvin, this is my grandmother's room, isn't it? And these really are her things?" I asked in a hushed voice, partly repelled but also charmed by the idea that her father had kept them there, waiting for her return.

Kelvin mewed.

"I don't think she would mind if I borrowed her clothes while I did laundry, do you? Especially not a nightgown," I said, reaching for the red flannel feedbag hanging from a hook on the back of the door. The slightly stiff gown was not attractive, but it would be warm.

Hesitating a moment, I took the slacks and sweater too. I would need something for tomorrow if the clothes didn't dry overnight.

The uncharacteristic jumble of shoes on the wardrobe floor were tempting since there were some flats and boots among the satin slippers, but Grandma had been a half-size smaller than I am and the shoes would probably pinch.

"Come out, Kelvin," I said and then noticed a small painting beside the wardrobe. It was a seagull on a rock, either deliberately done in the style of the impressionists or painted by someone who needed glasses. I squinted at the signature but couldn't make it out. Could this have been something my grandma painted? Or perhaps her mother? I would probably never know. I closed the door softly.

I looked in the tiny drawer of the bedside table, hoping for a forgotten picture or a note or anything that would tell me for sure that this really was my grandmother's bedroom, but there was nothing personal, not even perfume or a hairbrush. Maybe she had taken everything like that when she left. I liked that idea better than the one where someone—Kelvin or Harris perhaps—had gone through the house and systematically removed anything personal that had belonged to the previous occupants.

Furniture, drapery, linens, food—even the gun—were left behind, but pictures, letters, journals were all gone. The only item that contained any information was the Bible in the library.

Though the lack of personal items made the house seem more like it truly belonged only to me and not the dead, it reinforced the idea that I was being seduced into a beautiful trap, one that had been set and sprung many times before with other Wendovers. And someone didn't want me to know how my predecessors had felt about being caught in it.

The cat mewed and patted my ankle. It was nearing full dark and I hadn't brought a flashlight.

"Okay, Kelvin, let's go have a snack. I've worked hard today and cereal isn't cutting it. And I need some tea before bed."

A strong cup of tea is so prosaic that it denies even the most extraordinary things. It's why the British drink it in times of crisis. Maybe it would help me sleep.

Chapter 9

The sun winked out while I made tea. The light was somber and then it was gone, sunk in the sea, or so it seemed. Fortunately I had a flashlight on hand.

I read for a time and then tried to sleep, but the subconscious was restless about my tentative decision to move to the island, and bad dreams about my grandmother rowing desperately in a storm roused me again and again.

The last time I woke the cat was gone and my door was ajar, a slice of deeper darkness in the shadowy room. The doors in the bedrooms were latched rather than knobbed, so it was possible that the cat had opened it on his own, but my hands shook as I reached for my flashlight and switched it on. It helped to have light, but there was a large part of me that was afraid of the dark—at least the dark in that house—and it did not place much confidence in my plastic device to protect me from it. It was embarrassing, but the rational conviction I used every day of my life was ready to abdicate to supernatural terror. One clanking chain, one mournful wail, and I would forget that I didn't believe in ghosts and run screaming into the night.

There was a violent gust of wind and a blast of air from the chimney that scattered soot across the floor. Then it reversed itself and it felt as if all the air was sucked out of the room, making the bed curtains sway. The house's ghostly larynx moaned. I had heard of things like this happening in hurricanes and tornadoes, but we weren't having a violent storm. This was just the usual night rain with the standard collision of clouds that led to distant lighting. I needed to ignore the trilling of my nerves, which were not doing the usual low thrum of sensible concern at strange weather, but letting off an irrational screech from the highest register reserved for supernatural phenomenon.

Something wasn't right. I got out of bed. My borrowed nightgown was warm, but it could not chase away the cold of predawn fear. A glance at the window showed me it was later than I thought. There was a pencil-thin squiggle of light showing between the clouds. Not true dawn yet, but the sun rose quickly over the water where there were no mountains or trees to delay it.

Down the stairs I went, wasting no time with creeping. Nor did I look at the front door for fear that I might just keep heading that way and not stop until I was at Ben's house. Instead I turned left at the hall and headed for the kitchen and then right to the chimney where the basement door was concealed.

The door was closed. Bolted. This was a tremendous relief. But the cat was mewling loudly, using both front paws to claw at the door. Cold seeped over the gap at the sill and grasped my toes. I could smell the sea. It was the same current that I had felt and smelled that first night. It tasted of ocean and something more pungent.

"What the...." But my brain could only regurgitate the suggestion of a ghost in the basement, so I stopped asking it questions.

Instead I sat down on the oaken settle across the room and waited for the sun to come up. Kelvin came and lay beside me, staring fixedly at the bolted door.

An hour later, fortified with a cup of tea and dressed in Grandma's dungarees, I went back to the basement door. It did not surprise me that Kelvin was still waiting there, still staring.

Anger had mostly replaced fear, but it took courage to pull back the bolt and open the door on the damp darkness. I had two flashlights with me. One I would hang as a lantern and the other I would use as it had been intended. Night was over and the sun was up. Everything would be fine.

The basement was, as ever, empty of obvious life—no new cobwebs, no mouse droppings, nothing to suggest that Kelvin and I were not utterly alone. There was, however, a scent clutching at the now still air and occasionally tweaking my nose. It wasn't the wholesome smell of the ocean either. It smelled vaguely like a distillery I had visited in Scotland on one of those seven countries in seven days tours I had taken right after college.

It was probably unattractive, but I sniffed and sniffed, imitating a bloodhound. My nose led me to the locked cupboard and I knelt down and inhaled at the crack. That was where the smell came from. No longer in the mood to hunt for keys or secret latches, I went and got a crowbar. I used it forcefully on the heavy panel, irritation lending me strength. The door popped open with a screech and something heavy hit the floor. The wobbling light showed me the latching mechanism on the inside was intact, but the screws had rusted and popped free of the wood when I pried it open. Even metal could be defeated by the damp salt air.

Exhaling, I turned the flashlight into the cupboard and immediately spotted a gap in the back wall. It was only a little surprising to find a sliding panel and behind that a short stair and then a downward sloping tunnel which I could barely see while leaning into the closet. The chisel marks on the stone walls and the wooden steps showed me the tunnel was manmade, or at least man-modified. I crouched again and shone my light around a bit, pretending to examine the footprints on the steps while considering what to do next.

One kind of woman—a smarter or more timid or less annoyed one—might close the door, wedge a chair against it, and go call Harris or the police.

Except, was that smart? Harris had known my great-grandfather very well. Was he truly ignorant of the tunnel? Or had he failed to mention it because it could give me a distaste of Wendover House?

Had he failed to mention it because he was using it for some reason, a reason he didn't want me to know anything about?

And what could I say to Bryson or Everett Sands if I called? Having a tunnel in one's basement was not a police matter. Not unless someone was using it and I had no proof of that. Not yet.

Anyway, it was probably shutting the barn door after the horse was gone. Whoever had been here was probably long gone. There had been days—or at least nights—for them to learn that a new person was in the house and that I was being bothered enough by noises in the basement to put a lock on the door and ask questions about a sea cave.

"Oh, what the hell."

I stepped through the cupboard. It was a relief to find Kelvin padding along beside me in a most relaxed manner.

"Reow," he said encouragingly, happy that I had finally gotten the message.

Fear and irritation went away. I had stepped through the looking glass and into history. I had a hidden tunnel in my basement! This was great! I didn't know anyone who had a hidden tunnel.

The smell of booze was strong in the air, though it grew weaker as I got closer to the mouth of the small cave which I also had expected to find. About ten feet in from the opening there was a sort of winch with a broken cable bolted to the slanting floor. The end had frayed, parting the metal strands. The break looked recent. There was rust on the rest of the cable but the ends were still shiny.

What was a surprise were the half dozen barrels still in the cave, one of which was broken open. It was the contents which were perfuming the restless breeze that breathed in and out with the noisy waves, splashing at the cave's narrow mouth as they did their best to get inside. The other barrels were set up on ledges above the water line. The watermarks showed that the cave did not submerge completely at high tide. That there were still puddles of booze left meant someone had visited me last night after the tide had turned. That was doubtless what had roused the cat.

"Kelvin, don't drink that!" I scolded as the cat sniffed at a golden puddle, but my brain was busy trying to assimilate what it was seeing.

Someone was using my cave to hide barrels of liquor. Surely that meant smuggling. Why else risk trespassing and hiding the casks in so inconvenient a place? And this enterprise wasn't anything recent either. This cave had been here for a long time, long enough for certain barnacles and plants to attach themselves to the walls. It might even be the very cave used by the smuggler who had married my ancestress.

Was this why Grandma had left? Because her father was smuggling booze—and who knew what else—into the country? Had he expected her to do the same? Surely there was some record of this cave in some archive, somewhere.

I needed a computer with internet access and went to see if Ben had one.

"Come on Kelvin. We'll come back later."

* * *

"I can do you one better, if it's information on whisky smuggling that you want," Ben said enthusiastically when I explained my desire for a computer, though not about the sea cave and its booty. I had decided to hold that back for the time being. "As I told you, I've been doing research on smuggling and have pretty much read everything in the historical society archives. Uh—you don't mind a lecture? It would be faster than having you read my notes."

"Please feel free to core dump. Tell me all about bootlegging."

"You know not what you ask," he said with a grin that was positively boyish. "In the old days, rum-running—bootlegging— was about breaking the laws of prohibition in the U.S. And it still is, at least in as much as certain types of alcohol are still prohibited from legitimate trade, though alcohol consumption is allowed in most places. Then, as now, one of the main places where alcohol was smuggled from was Canada."

I nodded.

"I have a theory that these islands were used as a kind of base of operations because of their territory being in dispute. In fact, after I read about your piratical ancestor I decided to buy the house here. It's a great place for writing undisturbed." He cleared his throat and waited. I couldn't think what to say but nodded encouragingly.

"I can see that."

"Okay. As a for instance, small amounts of Canadian whisky could be legally brought into the coast guard and menial staff who manned the lighthouse. And once the ship was here, other cargo could be conveniently unloaded under the cover of night."

Ben gestured me into a chair beside his desk. It was a bit tatty but very comfortable.

"These rum-runners were an ingenious bunch. There was one smuggler who installed fish pens in the bottom of his ship to carry as much liquor as possible. He would put in at Goose Haven, making a legitimate delivery of fish, but then would leave a huge shipment somewhere on the islands to be picked up by land-smugglers when they came to buy fish or clams or whatever. They probably picked rainy nights so there would be fewer witnesses. A little rain wouldn't deter these guys." I nodded again. "Land-runners from the mainland would then come and retrieve supplies at the port and smuggle them deeper into the United States. I haven't figured out who was behind it—the money guys, I mean. But I can make some guesses."

He was the most animated I had ever seen him.

"Do you think that could be going on today?" I asked. "I mean, prohibition is over, so why take the risk?"

"I know it's going on today, though cigarettes and marijuana are the bigger illegal imports."

"Why? I mean why smuggle booze?" I insisted, not wanting to get off topic. "Is there still money in it?"

"Probably. Where there is demand there will be supply."

"But is there demand?"

"Of course. Canadian whisky is an indigenous product to Canada that, while satisfying all the laws of Canadian manufacture, does not meet U.S. standards for rye whiskey." I must have looked blank because he went on more slowly. "It is a common misconception that Canadian whiskies are primarily made using rye. Mostly they are made with corn. In their defense, they are all aged at least three years. There is no requirement for aging in the U.S., so one can argue about which is the better product. But that is an aesthetic rather than a legal distinction."

"Wait. Canadian rye whisky isn't made with rye—it's made with corn? And this is considered bad?"

"Mostly correct. The use of rye grain is not dictated by law in Canada, and whisky products of all grain types are often generically referred to as 'rye whisky.' The U.S. objects to this designation as misleading however and has strict laws about how much rye must be used in a blended whiskey."

"Okay. I suppose it really makes a difference in the flavor and people get to liking a particular kind of drink?" I thought of friends who liked Coke but wouldn't touch Pepsi.

"Yes. And the cost varies, of course, but Canadian whisky is usually cheaper than its American counterpart. Let me demonstrate the differences. That's the best way to understand." Ben went to a cupboard and got out four short glasses. This was followed by four bottles of varying shape and color. "I am going to pour you some whiskies. One is Canadian, one is a United States rye whiskey, one is Scottish, and one is Irish whiskey—that is spelled with an e-y, by the way. The Irish and Scottish whiskies taste substantially different. They are the parent drink though, so one should know about them."

I tried not to grimace. I was ignorant about whisky because I didn't like it at all, but I didn't want to stifle Ben's ever-growing enthusiasm and steady flow of information.

"The Irish whiskey first," he said handing me a glass with a very small amount in the bottom. Obviously he was serious about this being a taste and nothing more. "This is a single malt whiskey and has been distilled three times. It's very smooth."

I sniffed it. Whiskey, kind of like what I had smelled in the tunnel. I forced myself to take a sip and was pleasantly surprised. I didn't like it, but I didn't feel as though my teeth had been etched with acid.

"Not bad," I said and got an approving smile.

"Now for a Scottish whisky. Again, it is a single malt. Notice the peat. There is almost a flavor of smoke. It's my favorite," he confessed. "Aged in oak barrels."

The taste was very different, not as sweet and I didn't like it at all. It was like sucking ashes.

"I can taste the difference," I said diplomatically, setting the glass on the desk.

"Now, the American. This won't have the smoky flavor because fire wasn't used on the rye and wheat."

"It's sweeter," I said after I had dipped my numbed tongue in it. "I like it better." But not much.

Ben nodded. "It's probably more what you are used to. Now try the Canadian. This is a whisky intended for a Canadian market. It would not be imported into the U.S."

I accepted the last glass, glad we had reached the end of the bottles. I was beginning to feel a little woozy. Hard liquor has never been my friend and a very little of it went a long way.

"It's lighter," he said. "Fewer layers of flavors. Simple."

"Almost fruity," I agreed. "I like this best of all."

"So do a lot of Americans," he said wryly, no doubt decrying our unsophisticated palates.

"And you said this one isn't imported into the U.S.?"

"Not legally. And it is less expensive than other brands. A lot less expensive, especially in bulk."

"Well, I guess I see why someone might smuggle it in."

"Yes. And why they would put it in new bottles before serving it in pubs and inns and chowder houses."

Hearing a new note in his voice, I looked up at Ben.

"Like Mike's Chowder House or the Great Goose Public Inn?" I asked.

"Exactly like that."

"Oh." I tried to think, but the whisky was getting in the way. "Well, this is food for thought." I made another stab at making the brain cells function but it was hard going. I was beginning to feel very sleepy. "Do Bryson and Everett know about this?"

"Oh, I should think so. They both drink it regularly."

"Hm."

"Do you still want to use my computer? You're welcome."

"No thanks, at least not right now. I think what I need is a nap. I'm not used to drinking."

Ben was beginning to smile again.

"Can you get home by yourself?"

"Please. There is only one path. If I go the wrong way I'll fall into the ocean and that will tell me to stop."

"Nevertheless, I will walk you home. It's time to stretch my legs anyway." He offered me a hand and pulled me to my feet. I hated to admit that the help was welcome. Booze and a lack of sleep were a bad combination.

"So, is your new book about smuggling?"

He hesitated and then seemed to give a mental shrug.

"Yes, only not about smuggling booze. In my story the bad guys are trafficking in humans."

"Oh. That's bad. I'd rather have booze. I mean, in real life. Less tragedy that way."

"True, but far less literary drama," he answered, grinning as he opened the door. "Someday I would like to write a historical novel about rum-runners."

83

We stepped out and were greeted with a gust of wind and a view of gathering clouds.

"More rain?" I asked the sky. "This is summer, for heavensake. Can't we have one clear night?"

"It's summer but it's also Little Goose. I am surprised the whole island isn't lost to moss and mildew."

"I will begin to mildew if my clothes don't dry before it starts raining."

Chapter 10

I had a short nap. The afternoon was dreary when I woke and I felt no inclination to spend it cleaning the cellar, though I did make sure the cupboard door was secured with a nail before going back upstairs for the night.

My brain was busy chewing on the morning's discovery. I asked myself why I hadn't told Ben about the tunnel and the booze, but couldn't come up with an answer. Except that he seemed to know a lot about smuggling, had had ample time to get to know my great-grandfather, and might still be involved with the smugglers.

Not that he would be doing this full time, I assured myself. Probably it would just be research for a book, or something, but I didn't want the smugglers to be made aware that I had found their tunnel and the rest of their stash. Ben wouldn't hurt me—I was pretty sure—but the fact remained that smuggling is illegal and someone could end up in jail if this went public. Criminals tended not to like this. It seemed far safer to let them finish removing their goods in peace and to leave them in ignorance of the fact that I was on to their illegal import business.

And perhaps once the smugglers were gone, the tunnel's existence could be made remunerative in some way or another. After all, I was a reporter. Why couldn't I go freelance with the story of modern smuggling? I would bring my phone down in the morning and take a picture of the barrels. Surely someone somewhere would be interested enough to pay for this.

Or was exposing this story too dangerous? Too … rude? Or at least insulting to local custom?

I shook my head and made some tea.

Maybe I should have been more alarmed about crimes being committed by a person or persons unknown, but I just couldn't get as worked up over whisky as I would cocaine or Ben's hopefully mythical slave-trading. Most of my annoyance—now that I knew the causes of the night disturbances were manmade—was that I had had so many anxious, sleepless nights at the smuggler's hands.

Not that disturbing me had been intentional. Far from it. They were clearing out and I would be left in peace hereafter.

Or would I? If I did nothing, would they begin using the cave again the next time they had a shipment that needed storing? If they did, was that bad? What if they decided to bribe me into cooperation—offered a sort of rental agreement? It could be worth a lot of money. Would I take it? Involve myself in something illegal? I tried to imagine what my grandmother would do in my situation.

It was gloomy to contemplate, but looking at things realistically, my life was about half over. And what did I have to show for it? Until Kelvin had died and left me his home I had had a broken-down business and an apartment I was about to lose because it was being converted to condominiums.

I had no family, no sense even of what my family had been. I had been feeling rootless and discontent. I didn't have any real anchors in the community I'd moved back to when I inherited the newspaper because Grandma Mac and my parents had not been "joiners." There were no long-standing civic connections, no social clubs, not even close friends left from childhood, and only the two employees that came with Grandma Mac's business.

But now? Well, I still had no family, but I had a pre-existing place in the community if I chose to assume it. No one would question my past. I was the Wendover heir and all I had to do was live in this house. And it was a beautiful home. I had enough money to sleep nights without worry—once the smugglers were gone. I had a personable neighbor with shared interests, a chance at friends. And I had a cat who needed me.

Weighed against that was the knowledge that my property was being used for something illegal—something my grandmother had probably hated enough to run away from. And the trespassers abusing my hospitality were probably people I knew.

Like my personable neighbor, or my attorney.

"Enough," I said as I stopped to stare out the window for what felt like the hundredth time.

I needed distracting and recalled the book in the library about witchcraft in Maine. It was the perfect time to give it a try. Maybe witches would be more interesting than smugglers.

Kelvin joined me in the library and I built a small fire. We settled into an armchair and put our feet up on the ottoman.

The font was hard to read and the print dense, the prose turgid. But the subject was sensational enough to encourage me to the labor of reading. It was nice to learn in the preface that no one had ever been executed for practicing witchcraft in Maine. Since the book began on this hopeful note, I thought that maybe I was ready for a bit of sensational reading though the wind was clearly rising outside and we would be having another storm.

However, it turned out that this claim of forbearance was a slight misstatement. There had been two executions in what is now Maine when it was still part of Massachusetts. The name of one of the persecutors caught my eye.

I should have closed the book at this point, but I got caught up in the story of Colonel Sands and the black witch. She was seventeen and beautiful, but never given a name, which is typical, as women were so often dismissed historically. The accused creature *lived with her aunt in a cabin where the black rocks of the island set a guard against the white man's coming*, or so the rather bad poem immortalizing the trial said.

Brought before the heartless colonel, who had probably been having an affair with the accused witch and was trying to deny the connection, the usual accusations of broom-riding and crop-killing ensued. The poor woman was gagged throughout the proceedings so that *she would not lay hurtful spells upon the witnesses*—and not mention her affair with Sands. Not so amazingly, she was found guilty and judgment was passed: *Thou shalt be bound in thine own house on the evil island, and we will burn the shameful whole to ash and you with it.*

Fortunately, our ancestors were not barbarians. The burning was mere poetic license and anyway, why destroy a perfectly good cabin that someone else could use as soon as the aunt was gotten rid of? They decided to hang her instead. As the noose was placed around her delicate neck, she uttered a last curse: *Jonathan Sands, listen to these words, the last my mouth shall utter. In the spirit of the only true and living God I speak thee. Tremble, for you will soon die. Over your grave they will erect a stone that all may know where the bones of the cowardly Jonathan Sands are moldering. But listen, all ye people, that your descendants may know the truth. Upon that stone will appear the imprint of my raised hand, and for*

*an eternity after your accursed names have perished from the
earth, the people will come from afar to view the fulfillment of this
prophecy and will say: 'There lies the man who murdered an
innocent woman.' Remember these words well, Jonathan Sands,
remember me.*

And sure enough, Sands died in an accident shortly thereafter
and his widow erected a granite headstone over his grave. Almost
at once a handprint appeared, obscuring Winston's name. The
stone was replaced, but again a mark in the shape of a hand blotted
out his name. This time they left the stone alone.

If it had been me, I would have come up with a better curse. I
mean, if you are calling down the wrath of something all-powerful,
let's do a good and thorough job of cursing. You know, think of
Job and all his afflictions. But I guess you do what you can and
maybe this was all she could think of in what had to be a very
stressful moment.

The rest of the book was less exciting. Other women were
"questioned" for being witches, but this was the only execution in
the islands. There seemed to be a real suspicion among the Puritans
for people who lived on the northern frontiers and tiny islands off
the coast who might have had dealings with the Indian tribes who
were known conjurers and sorcerers and who regularly had
congress with demons. People like my ancestor, Abercrombie
Wendover. I could only sigh over the ignorance of these long-dead
Puritans and pity them for their irrational and unnecessary fears.

I had thought that the story was out of my head by the time I
made dinner and went to bed, but my dreams that night were
troubled. I dreamed of a headstone with a bloody handprint on it,
but the stone did not belong to Colonel Sands. The slightly
obscured name read *Kelvin Wendover.*

The next morning I woke with the intention of discovering
where Kelvin was buried. I would pay my respects, bring some
flowers. Then I was going up to the attic and tearing it apart. There
had to be some pictures, some paintings, some diaries, or personal
mementos of my ancestors.

However, the best laid plans of mice and men and all that. I
had just climbed out of the bathtub when there was a knock on the

door. I scrambled into my borrowed clothes, which were inclined to stick on the damp patches and roll annoyingly in the hardest to reach locations.

Expecting it was Ben, or perhaps Harris, I was shocked speechless to find Jack, a pair of crutches and a duffel bag sheltering on my doorstep.

"Dear God!" I said before being enveloped in a hug. A cool wind rushed over my bare feet as I was pulled onto tiptoes.

I started laughing, partly from shock but partly from relief.

"You smell like mothballs and look like Katherine Hepburn," he said.

"What are you doing here? How are you here? You must have left right after we got off the phone."

"Almost," he admitted, letting me back far enough to look at my face. "I have been so damned worried since I talked to you. Do you know how crazy you sounded?"

"I've been worried too," I admitted. "But, Jack, it's just gotten even weirder and more awesome since then."

"Weirder?"

"Yes, I'll tell you, but come in first. Have you had breakfast?" I bent to take his duffel. It was heavier than my little suitcase.

"Not as such. I ate things in airports," he said, looking around with wide eyes as he came through the foyer and into the front parlor. I knew he was impressed. *I* was still impressed and I had had several days to get used to the house. "Wow. This is like something from a museum—only more real. More lived in."

"I know. Wait until you see the kitchen. The stove is a hoot."

"I'm glad you are taking it so well. You sounded rather stressed when we talked the other night."

"I was stressed. But that's when I thought maybe I had ghosts."

"Ghosts?" He stared at me.

"Yes, but I was wrong. It's much better than that. So, who brought you over to the island?" I asked, setting down his duffel at the foot of the stairs and leading the way to the kitchen. "There's no ferry today."

"Um—someone called Bryson Sands gave me a lift. He was coming to pay a call on your novelist neighbor. I gather they have a weekly poker game." Jack thumped along behind me. He wasn't hurrying and I didn't blame him. There was a lot to see.

"Really? That is interesting. Bryson is one of the two brother police officers that are the law on the islands. He's the more personable of the two. Here, sit on the settle and I'll make some breakfast. Do eggs sound okay? I have lots of eggs."

"Sure." Jack lifted his cast up onto the bench and sighed with pleasure.

There was a meow at the back door and I let Kelvin in. The cat paused with one paw raised, studied Jack for a moment, and then decided that he was okay, even if he and his leg were taking up the whole settle. Kelvin came forward, rubbed once at Jack's undamaged limb, and then sauntered off to the pantry for a midmorning snack.

"So, you don't have ghosts?" Jack asked, staring at the cat. I was pretty sure that he was thinking of the similarities between Kelvin and the cats in some of the paintings. It was kind of disturbing until you realized that many cat characteristics bred true generation after generation—especially on an island with limited mating possibilities.

"No—at least they aren't what's been getting me up nights."

"That's good, I guess. What has been getting you up?"

I couldn't contain my smile.

"Smugglers."

Jack stared at me, not smiling.

"Smugglers? Like … *smugglers*?"

"Yes, smugglers are using my secret tunnel and sea cave to store illegal Canadian whisky. Or they were. They've been emptying it out night after night. I think it would be clear by now, except their winch broke. They'll need to bring in another."

Jack exhaled slowly.

"Maybe you should start at the beginning. You have a secret tunnel and a sea cave?"

"I do. I found them yesterday while I was cleaning the basement." Eggs forgotten, I perched on the very end of the settle and started telling Jack about the tunnel and the ins and outs of whisky importation laws.

90

Jack let me talk. I was fairly organized in my presentation so he didn't need to ask a lot of questions.

"So, you don't know who the smugglers are?"

"No. I have possible suspects—"

"Like your neighbor and the lawyer?" he guessed.

Yes, but I didn't like hearing this expressed aloud.

"And the police. At least, Ben says they have to know that the chowder house and other places are serving illegal liquor."

"But…. You're sure it's illegal? I mean, with the islands maybe belonging to Canada it could be legal, right?"

"It's a gray area," I conceded. "I think it's been unofficially decided that the lighthouse is Canadian but the rest is American. And for sure, anything that goes to the mainland is illegal."

"Wow. So what are you going to do about it?" he asked.

"I don't know. At least, I don't know if I'll tell anyone in an official capacity."

"Not tell?" Jack asked. He appeared baffled and disapproving.

"How can I when the local law is probably involved? And anyway, I suspect that my great-grandfather was in it up to his eyebrows. I bet it's why my grandma ran away." I didn't bring up the curse. It sounded stupid when a believer told the story. It would be worse if I explained it.

"So? Your great-grandfather is dead. He can't be prosecuted so what has this got to do with you reporting this? If you are worried about Bryson and his brother being involved, go to the ATF. The government will care, believe me. They don't like leaky borders and people smuggling anything over them."

"But…." I found I couldn't explain about the pressure of family history I was beginning to feel. Telling Jack I didn't want to tarnish the Wendover name seemed stupid, but the feeling persisted anyway. "Well, there is also the matter of not offending the neighbors."

"What?" He sounded incredulous.

"I want to live here, Jack. That means getting on with the locals. Smuggling whisky is kind of a tradition in these parts. Sending my neighbors to jail would not endear me to the community. Besides, word has gone out now that Kelvin—Great-grandpa Kelvin—is dead and a new person lives here now. If they

wanted to deal with me, I would have been approached already."
Probably. "Instead they are moving everything off the island in the
dead of night—which is kind of thoughtful, if you think about it
the right way."

"Are you crazy?" he asked, and then proceeded to explain my
advanced insanity.

I nodded sympathetically while he lectured and went to fix
him some eggs and toast, hoping breakfast would calm him.

"You aren't listening, are you?" he finally asked.

"I'm listening."

"No, you're—what are you doing?"

"I don't have a toaster, so I have to do the bread over a flame.
It's tricky—harder than doing marshmallows."

"Tess, what are you thinking?" he sounded despairing. "I've
never known what you're thinking. From day one you were a
closed book. And I can't help but feel a little responsible about
this."

"Whatever for?" I asked, surprised.

"We didn't part on the best terms and before I could make
things right I went and broke my leg. Next thing, I hear you're in
Maine, on some island, and have smugglers in your basement
which you don't plan to do anything about. So, I ask again, what
are you thinking?"

"I'm thinking that I am so glad to see you," I said earnestly,
trying to reassure him. "It's like I've been visiting some foreign
land, which I guess this is, and nothing feels quite right. It's—it's
mostly wonderful here but not what I'm used to. I mean, for one
thing, absolutely everyone knows more about my family than I do.
That's weird, isn't it? So it is great to see a familiar face. One I
know I can trust. One that isn't superstitious either. We have a lot
of superstitious people around here."

I put toast on the plates and scooped up the scrambled eggs
from the frying pan.

"Let's go into the breakfast room. It's nice. The dining room
is a little overwhelming."

"Okay," he said, finally relaxing. I was pretty sure that Jack
hadn't given up on trying to persuade me to do something about
the smugglers, but he was willing to bide his time while he won me

over with reason. "And then I want to see your tunnel and the cave. It sounds like something out of Stevenson."

"Or the Hardy Boys," I agreed, carrying both plates while Jack dealt with the crutches. "It's really amazing. We need to go before high tide though, or we won't be able to make it all the way to the cave."

"The eggs are great," Jack said a few minutes later. "I hadn't realized I was so hungry."

"It's the sea air," I said without thinking. "It gives you an appetite."

Jack put his fork down.

"Tess, you don't think that, lost in the euphoria of inheriting this insanely beautiful house on a romantic island with an exotic neighbor and smugglers in the basement, you maybe aren't overestimating your chances of happiness living here?"

"What am I, Nostradamus?" I sighed, ashamed at being snappish, especially when Jack had come all the way to see me. "Maybe. But it *is* insanely beautiful and romantic. People are ready to accept me too. I can be a Wendover from Little Goose. And it isn't like I've been happy in Minnesota, not since—well, ever. We just weren't a good fit. Too many people take intelligence as an insult—a trick that I'm playing on them. I know this is a small town too, but it feels very different."

Jack looked sympathetic.

"Anyway," I accused with a grin, "you're leaving town too. What makes you think you'll like living somewhere else either?"

"Okay—*pax*. I'll suspend my hasty judgment about your island. Let's go see your secret tunnel."

"There are some stairs, can you manage them?"

"Sure, if I go slow."

Chapter 11

I had a bad moment, watching Jack negotiate the basement stairs. I tried to talk him out of exploring the tunnel, but he was adamant. Perhaps he wanted to assure himself that I wasn't hallucinating. I have to admit, my story was a wild one.

We made it to the bottom steps without incident and I went to the cupboard and pulled out my nail that was serving as a bolt. I opened the door slowly. I wasn't being theatrical, just cautious. A shriek from the hinges would have added to the eerie atmosphere, but the door and the cupboard's back panel opened without a sound.

"This is definitely designed for privacy," Jack said softly.

"Alcohol was illegal back then," I pointed out, also just above a whisper. "A smart man would plan things carefully."

The hidden staircase was solid enough but creaked under our combined weight as we torqued it from side to side with each cautious step. I was able to walk quietly, but Jack's crutches made a certain amount of noise. That shouldn't have bothered me since logic said we were alone. Still I wished that we were able to be a little quieter. The distant slushing of waves couldn't mask the sound of our approach.

The tunnel slope wasn't terribly steep and it wasn't slippery, but I could see that Jack was tiring by the time we reached the cave. As I had expected, everything was still in place though much of the whisky smell had dissipated.

"Amazing. I feel like I'm in a Hardy Boys adventure—The Mystery of the Smugglers' Cave or something."

"No, The Secret Stairs," I countered. "The other is too much of a giveaway for a title. It wouldn't do to step on the punch line."

Jack grinned and I remembered why I had agreed to date him.

Things got suddenly darker and a strong gust of wind whirled into the cavern. It carried the smell of storm.

"Here we go again," I muttered.

"Hm," Jack grunted and started for the mouth of the cave. "This isn't exactly the safest place for docking. I wonder—yes. Here's a ring. They could tie a boat off here if the tide were high enough."

I looked down at a circle of heavy iron just inside the cave that had rusted the same shade as the rock it was bolted into.

Another blast of wind hit us. We crept out a little further on the ledge and looked out of the fissure at the sky, which was frankly apocalyptic. All it needed was a funnel cloud to make it the perfect backdrop for a disaster film. The waves heaved and the rising wind slapped us around in an unfriendly manner. The birds nesting in the cliffs were shrill with unhappiness. Lighting struck near Goose Haven, followed almost immediately by thunder.

Jack whistled as he ducked back inside.

"It does this every night," I said, though truthfully this looked more dire than usual. "Let's go build a fire and break out the whisky." I started to laugh. "Which is probably smuggled. I'll make some split-pea soup for dinner."

"Well, it's a safe bet that your smuggler friends won't be around this evening." He sounded relieved. "No sane person would be out in this."

"Probably not," I agreed and then shivered. It was mostly the growing cold, but I had one of my rare flashes of imagination about what it would be like to be out on the water on such a night. I'd rather face a houseful of ghosts then step a single toe into a boat during a bad storm. I hoped the smugglers were as sensible.

More lightning and a prolonged scream of wind raced past us. I said a silent prayer that the house kept its grip on the tilted island. After all, it wasn't New Year's Eve and there was a Wendover—or at least a facsimile thereof—in residence. We should be safe.

* * *

My phone rang just before seven and I rushed upstairs to retrieve it from the bedside table where it had been abandoned. It was Harris letting me know that the electrician would be out the day after next, or sooner, if the storm settled. The news was cheering. Hopefully the smugglers would have their whisky out of the cave by the time Mr. Benson was ready to begin the actual work in the basement so there would be no chance of the parties meeting.

When I returned to the parlor I found Jack was asleep. The early dark brought by the storm coupled with soup and the warm fire—and Kelvin's whisky—had done its work.

As I hadn't touched the whisky, I was not so much sleepy as contemplative. My subconscious had been at work, thinking about what Jack had said while we were down in the cave. It had gathered its data and presented me with its conclusions as I draped a quilt over Jack and tucked him into his easy chair. He looked very comfy with his leg up on the ottoman and the firelight playing over his face.

Intuition said that the smugglers probably wouldn't want to risk traveling any distance at sea on such a night, especially once their boats were weighed down with hundreds of gallons of whisky and riding low in the water. But what if the smuggler was already on the island? Would it be so hard to move their boat around to the cave during a lull in the storm, load it, and then go back to the dock? In the morning, after the gale burned out, they could leave openly with no one the wiser.

The wind died down. By eight it was almost calm. It came as no great shock when Kelvin got up from his nest on the settee and trotted for the kitchen. I followed him straight to the basement door where he was busy scratching at the panels. As had happened on other nights, I could feel a current of cold air creeping through the gap at the bottom of the door.

So, they had come back and for some reason opened the cupboard door. The only question was who it was who played smuggler. It could be Bryson—with or without Ben. It might also be Everett. After all, he "sometimes kept company with Mary Cory"—who had been very quick to warn me away from searching for a sea cave. If her employer was an invalid, he might not know what was going on.

And there was nothing to say it wasn't Harris. His call had sounded awfully clear and he had been tight with my great-grandfather. He knew Mary Cory very well and, though I didn't like to think it, he and Ben might only be pretending not to get along. I liked both men, but there was no way to know if their morals were a bit smudged. Or a lot smudged.

Kelvin objected to being shut in the pantry, but I decided his presence wasn't needed. I felt a little anxious so it seemed wise to stop by the library and pick up Kelvin's gun. My great-grandfather had had it for a reason, and this looked to be the general outline of a good reason for having a firearm.

I took a flashlight as well but didn't need it for long once I was down the stairs and through the cupboard, which had blown open. They had bright lanterns in the cave and the damp walls reflected the light nicely.

There were two voices veering up the tunnel. Male, I thought, but they were distorted and I couldn't make out their words until I was almost in the cavern.

"Move, you bejezurdly barrel!"

I peered around the corner with a slowness that would have angered a tortoise, giving my eyes time to get over their dazzlement. The first dripping back I saw belonged to Everett Sands. He was muscling another barrel to the cavern entrance without benefit of a handcart or sledge. About half of the casks were already gone.

His presence wasn't entirely unexpected, but still he was my least favorite of the candidates I had imagined for the role of villain. He was a multidimensional chameleon—a policeman and a smuggler and who knew what else. He was also unfriendly.

Truthfully I felt trepidation at being discovered by him and was ready to scurry away.

But then there was a muffled shout and large hands appeared at the mouth of the cave. I held my breath, waiting to see who was there and hoping passionately that it wasn't Harris who was helping Everett. It was something of a relief when Bryson Sands hauled himself inside. His hair was dark with rain and he looked cold and exasperated.

I drew back deeper into the shadows and listened as they talked logistics. Kelvin's gun was heavy in my hand, but I was glad to have it.

So, I knew who was smuggling whisky into Goose Haven. It was enough for the time being, I decided. I liked Bryson and I think he liked me, but I wasn't insane. There was no way that I was going to confront the brothers and ask about their plans. Though not usually imaginative, I had a frightening vision of Everett shoving me out of the cave and into the sea, which I could hear bubbling like a cauldron under the lashing wind. Bryson might not like it, but Everett was his brother and both of them had a lot to lose.

    No, I was going back upstairs, bolting the basement door, and hunkering in by the fire with my sleeping guest. It would take some effort, but I was going to do my best to cultivate a taste for my great-grandfather's whisky. If Jack woke I would take him upstairs and we would act like civilized people and sleep in beds, but if he didn't, I was fine with feeding the fire and napping on the other settee until dawn.

Chapter 12

Jack was hung over, and after a plain breakfast of oatmeal he decided that he would like to sit in the sun in the backyard and enjoy the morning calm while his pain pill did its work. As usual, day dawned with bright innocence, ignorant of the storm the night before. After using an aging rake to scrape away most of the slippery slime from the flagstones, which I noticed were arranged in the same pattern as the floor of the basement, I left him with a cup of tea and an Adirondack chair that we dragged off the porch and out into the sun.

During the long night I had had a lot of time to think about all kinds of things. Bryson and Everett had, of course, been on my mind for a portion of the night, but after midnight had come and gone, I had gotten to thinking about the things in the attic—the burned furniture and the clothes which were probably my great-grandmother's. I also thought about the oddly placed windows and why the room had felt so crowded. By the time dawn was stirring, I was sure that I had an answer for the oddities.

Jack would have come with me had I asked him, but the stairs were steep and narrow, and I had a feeling that I might not like what I was about to find. If it was anything personal or painful—or just plain weird—I didn't want any witnesses to my reaction. This was a private moment between me and my family's ghosts.

Kelvin and I went back to the attic and walked directly to the wall that had troubled me before. Now I knew why the proportions looked wrong. To the right and to the left were outside walls with windows. In this style of house, windows in pairs were usually spaced equidistant in the wall, causing a pleasing symmetry. But one window on each side appeared off by about four feet. And, of course, they weren't misplaced at all. It wasn't the windows that were off. The builders were not clumsy. There had been an addition to the room, a new wall. And it wasn't that old. I could still smell the lumber.

It took some effort to move the wardrobe full of stuffed, rotting animals, but I found a small, hidden door just where I expected it to be. It took some forcing but eventually I was able to open it far enough to squeeze through the opening.

The room beyond was closet-sized and the whitewashed outside walls were blackened in places with what I suspected was smoke damage from a leaking chimney. Or maybe from the fire in the old house. There was only one small window but the attic was bright enough that extra light spilled around me and into the room and it made up for the deficit.

Here were the missing portraits of my family, hung haphazardly on the walls and especially eerie in that dim light because they all did look like me and a lot of them had cats that looked like Kelvin. Taken altogether, they looked like a coven of constipated witches. The main difference between us was that they all looked very grim. Of course, in that moment, I probably wasn't smiling either, so maybe the match was closer than I thought.

There was a harp up there as well. It had my grandmother's name carved on it in crude letters which I suspected she had done herself. Had she liked playing it? Or was this something her father forced her to do because of that idiot legend Harris had mentioned? It might have been the latter since she never showed any inclination to play a musical instrument in the years I knew her.

Kelvin sneezed.

"Bless you."

There was a small table in the corner. I found a journal there along with several books of local history which I was sure would be instructive. I wasn't terribly surprised to discover it was my grandmother's diary.

Though I eventually wanted to read the whole thing, I turned to the final entry.

If I don't leave while my father still lives then I shall be forced by the others to stay. What will happen later I cannot guess, but I will not allow it to affect me any longer. My children, God willing I have them, shall not be bound by the curse either.

In spite of the trapped heat in the stuffy room, my flesh was chilled. Empathy was too weak a word for what I was feeling.

My grandmother hadn't run away from Little Goose because she didn't believe the crazy legend that haunted her father and made him demand that she stay. She had left because she *had* believed. And because others in Goose Haven believed too, and she would have been *forced by the others to stay* if she did not escape while she could.

I felt pity for the frightened girl she must have been.

Kelvin meowed and patted my leg.

"We'll go soon. Poor thing. I guess your family has been stuck here for a long time too."

Had my great-grandfather built this room and tried to hide the ugly truth of his family's misery away from himself? Maybe thinking that once out of sight he could forget his own imprisonment? It's what I would probably do, but I didn't think this room was here because of Kelvin's sensitivities. This felt more like something Harris would arrange. His search for an heir had been a long one. He had certainly had time to construct this chamber while he was looking for my grandmother, or more likely, her children. And it would be worth the effort to hide all this stuff, at least in his mind. He wanted the heir to stay—desperately, it seemed—and nothing could be allowed to interfere with that.

He couldn't bring himself to destroy family portraits or my grandmother's things though, not even her diary, which would probably tell me all kinds of stuff about the local cult, or whatever it was, that believed Wendovers had to stay on the island to keep the town from perishing. But knowing on some level that any rational person would reject both the legend and also any ties to a community that believed the insane story enough to imprison someone on the island, Harris had created a hiding place and stowed all the unattractive and betraying things in it.

He had overlooked my grandmother's clothes, maybe because of being in a hurry and he had forgotten to empty the wardrobe before I arrived, or perhaps because the clothing by itself didn't have anything to do with the damned legend and could be left in place for me to use.

"Damn it, Harris."

Now I knew two potentially dangerous things. The question was what I wanted to do about either one.

Jack's voice interrupted my thoughts.

"I'm in the attic!" I called down.

For half a minute I had an urge to close the door on the disturbing trove of family portraiture, but there was no way I could move the wardrobe back into place before Jack made it up the stairs.

I decided to compromise and tucked away my grandmother's diary. The portraits were quite distracting enough. I didn't need to bring up the whole island cult thing and get him started fussing again. Not that there wasn't reason for concern, but I hadn't made up my mind what I wanted to do. As crazy as it sounds to write this, I thought that I still wanted to live on the island.

Jack thumped to the door. He didn't squeeze into the small space but stuck his head inside.

"Good God!" he exclaimed.

I glanced at him. His face had color and he looked a lot more lively. His pills were clearly working.

"They look like a murder of crows," I said, opting to leave the witch metaphor out of the conversation.

"Were they Puritans? All that black clothing. I can't see any of them whooping it up at a church sociable."

"I can't either. Nor can I see any reason to take these paintings downstairs. I'm glad to have them as historical references, but there is no need to ruin one's appetite looking at their sour mugs."

"Are those books?" Jack asked. It figures he would notice. Jack is an avid reader.

"Yes. I thought I would bring them downstairs and have a look in more comfortable surroundings. I think that they are all local history—probably boring and full of lies. Why else relegate them to the attic? But I'll read them anyway." I started picking up the heavy tomes. I got about half of them and it didn't include my grandmother's journal. "This is enough for now. I'll get the rest later."

"Damn this leg. I wish I could help you more."

"You are helping," I said and meant it. "It's great to have you here. In fact … I hate to even ask, but how long can you stay?"

"Only till Friday," Jack said, politely closing the small door behind me. We had to dodge and dance to get by the wardrobe. "What's in here anyway? It's kind of smelly."

"Taxidermy gone awry," I said as he opened the door and took in all the shining eyes and snarling mouths.

"Ugh. Are you going to throw them out?"

"After I've looked them over and made sure none of them are stuffed with the family jewels—or that any of the animals is on some endangered or extinct species list that belongs in a museum."

"Oh. You're probably right. Your family seems…."

"Eccentric? Yes, I think they were." I started down the stairs. "Come on, Kelvin. You don't want to get stuck up here."

"Maybe I'll look through some of your books there. I bet they're fascinating."

I bet they were too. But I wasn't sure I wanted Jack reading them just yet.

"Okay. But first I want to check the cave." I knew this would distract him.

"Why?"

"I think the smugglers were back last night." I almost slipped and named names. "Kelvin was acting strange and scratching at the basement door. He's done that on other nights."

I did not admit to going downstairs to investigate.

"Are you kidding?" This was rhetorical. "Are they insane? The sea was crazy violent last night."

I wondered about their sanity too though the weather had calmed around eight. I could have explained my theory about the boat already being on the island but opted not to. Jack might want to go right down to the docks and investigate. I suspected Bryson and Everett's boats would be long gone by now, but why tempt disaster?

"Harris called about seven last night and he said the electrician would be out as soon as the sea calmed, so I would like to check on the whisky situation. The electrician will be bringing wires in through the basement so that the historic look of the house is preserved. It would be handy if the whisky was gone before he started work. If not, I'll have to seal the cupboard up tight and keep Mr. Benson away from the cave."

"Let's go look right now."

"Are you up to more stairs?" I asked.

"I feel fine. These pain pills are great."

I did some more thinking while we worked our way to the cave, which was blessedly empty. Even the broken winch was gone. This was a relief. I didn't like the idea of the Sands brothers visiting my basement, which they must have done to let the cat into the house that first night. I thought about how to go about arranging things so they wouldn't be tempted to use it again later if they had a need. The indirect approach sounded best.

"I bet Bryson is eating double donuts and coffee today," I muttered, thinking of the labor he and Everett had put in last night.

"What?" Jack asked.

"Nothing. I think that I would like you to meet Harris and Ben," I said, as we worked our way back upstairs. In spite of his super pill, Jack was beginning to look tired again.

"Why?" he asked bluntly.

"I want them to know there is an outside witness when I tell them about finding the cave. I won't mention that I saw the whisky. Just that I know the cave is there and that I am thinking of making it into a wine cellar or a bird sanctuary or something. Word will get out to the rest of the town quickly enough once they know that I know."

Jack thumped a couple more steps into the library and pulled out a chair.

"That isn't a bad idea. Subtle. This is tricky because you don't know who is smuggling."

I nodded.

"I'll ask the other neighbor too. Her name is Mary—she's actually the practical nurse for the owner of the other cottage, but he isn't mobile." She was also Everett's girlfriend. This would make the chance of word getting back to him immediately almost a certainty. "We'll call it a cocktail party. And that means I'll need cocktails and snacks. I had better call Miss Sibley and see if she has any cheese and crackers in the store. If not, I'll need to go to Goose Haven. Why don't you have a rest while I phone around and make arrangements."

"Okay. Confound this leg." He sat down carefully at the desk and reached for a book. It was on eighteenth-century maritime law. I patted his shoulder and went away.

Ben was pleased with the invitation and offered to call Mary for me since there was a lot of static on my phone that morning. Since Mary and I weren't the best of friends I agreed to the plan.

Harris sounded a bit winded when he answered the office phone, but was also pleased to be invited and I think a little relieved that he was to be included. He thoughtfully offered to bring over supplies. Since Miss Sibley was so hard of hearing and I quailed at the thought of making myself understood, I again agreed to deputize, suggesting cheese and crackers and a couple bottles of red and white wine.

A quick glance in the pantry showed me that I had an assortment of pickled things that I could use to supplement the cheese and crackers. It wouldn't be a party for the home and garden magazines, but it would do for the time being.

"We're all set," I told Jack who was standing in the backyard and staring at the smudged flagstones. I guess maritime law was not that engrossing.

"Good," he said absently. "You know, I feel like I should recognize this design. I've seen it somewhere."

"Me too. It's one of the many things I plan on looking up once I have power and my computer." Jack grunted. "Well, you enjoy the sun. I'm going to cut some flowers and give the parlor a dusting."

And take a look at the books I had brought down and hide any that made my family look too kooky. I didn't need Jack or anyone else reading them ahead of me.

My study of the books was perfunctory since I had to take a little time to shove some flowers in a vase and drag a cloth around the room. One book caught my eye because of the maze design in it. The rest seemed to be about sea trade routes and the predicted boring histories of saintly local families.

Jack came in looking for lunch before I had scanned more than a half dozen tomes.

"You know what that stonework out back reminds me of?" he asked, sounding pleased. "It's the yellow brick road from *The Wizard of Oz.*"

I smiled, but if the book I had looked at was right, it was a Native American symbol for the Four Ages of Man. Whether this was a good symbol or a bad one—or just decorative—I couldn't say. But it lent credence to the story about the island having belonged to the local tribe before Abercrombie moved here.

* * *

My guests arrived at seven. Clouds were gathering, but they remained thoughtfully distant and I thought that perhaps we were going to manage a night without rain. This sudden clearing had to infuriate the Sands brothers who had been working night after night in showers and wind.

It took only a moment to lay out a tray of nibbles and pour everyone some wine. We did a few moments of chitchat, Mary Cory even unbending enough to say welcome of Jack and ask about his leg.

After everyone had chewed a few crackers and sipped a bit of wine, I made my big announcement.

"I found something wonderful today—actually two wonderful things." Harris looked arrested, but Ben began to grin. Mary remained stone-faced. Jack's eyes were all over everyone. He was probably trying to pick out the smugglers.

"You found the cave!" Ben guessed.

"I did. It turns out that there is a tunnel leading from it to the basement. Of course, I don't plan on making this fact generally known, but I thought that you all would like to see it."

Harris managed to look both surprised and interested.

"I would certainly like to see it," he said politely.

"It isn't one of the wonders of the world or anything," I warned. "But it might make a nice wine cellar or something."

"Let's see it at once," Ben suggested, and so we got up and went downstairs again, even Jack, who had to be tired of making this trip.

The cave was admired for a minute or so. It looked more mysterious than it was when seen by the light of a single flashlight. I pointed out the iron ring and Ben, predictably, drew the right conclusions about its use.

Ben would have lingered but I shooed everyone upstairs. The cave was damp and getting cold.

"You said there were two things," Ben reminded me as we settled back into the parlor and I lit the fire.

"Yes. I also found a small room off of the attic and it was full of family portraits." I watched Harris and was not surprised to see him flush with guilt. "They were not an attractive lot and it quite depresses me that everyone sees my resemblance to them. Still, they are family and we don't get to choose our genetic destiny." I stood up and reached for my wine. "We can choose other things though."

I smiled at the room but turned my gaze back to Harris. I thought of all the people I had met and couldn't think that anyone except Harris and his parents, and perhaps a few people of that generation, actually believed the legend.

"And?" he prompted. "You've chosen something?"

"Yes. And I'm going to stay. I love the house. I've made new friends and hope to make more. And this isn't the eighteenth century. If I get lonely for fast food or want to see a movie, I can always hop the ferry to the mainland. It isn't like I'd be a prisoner here."

I don't think anyone but Harris took my meaning.

"I'm very glad," he said sincerely.

"As am I!" Ben said and I knew that both of them meant it, though for different reasons.

Mary added her congratulations but I don't think she was completely sincere about her happiness at acquiring a new neighbor.

"If I can get a flight on such short notice, I will fly back on Friday with Jack and start packing up my apartment. I have to make arrangements for the sale of the newspaper, but I don't think any of it will take long. I'll be back before winter. Hopefully before fall. Harris, will you mind dealing with the electrician while I'm gone?"

"Not at all."

I exhaled. "Good. And, though it is a long time off, I would like to invite everyone to a Christmas party. You too, Jack, if you can get away. And next time I will manage something better than pickled onions and crackers."

And I would have my grandmother's shotgun. Just in case.

About the Author

Melanie Jackson is the author of over 50 novels. If you enjoyed this story, please visit Melanie's author web site at www.melaniejackson.com.

eBooks by Melanie Jackson:

The Chloe Boston Mystery Series:
Moving Violation
The Pumpkin Thief
Death in a Turkey Town
Murder on Parade
Cupid's Revenge
Viva Lost Vegas
Death of a Dumb Bunny
Red, White and a Dog Named Blue
Haunted
The Great Pumpkin Caper
Beast of a Feast

The Butterscotch Jones Mystery Series
Due North
Big Bones
Gone South

Wildside Series
Outsiders
Courier
Still Life

The Book of Dreams Series:
The First Book of Dreams: Metropolis
The Second Book of Dreams: Meridian
The Third Book of Dreams: Destiny

Medicine Trilogy
Bad Medicine

Medicine Man
Knave of Hearts

Club Valhalla
Devil of Bodmin Moor
Devil of the Highlands
Devil in a Red Coat
Halloween
The Curiosity Shoppe (Sequel to A Curious Affair)
The Secret Staircase
Timeless
Nevermore: The Last Divine Book

23025647R00061

Made in the USA
Lexington, KY
26 May 2013